Publisher: Tom Kaczynski
Associate Publisher: Jordan Shiveley

Design: Tom Kaczynski
Production Assist: Jordan Shiveley

Translation: Marzena Sowa & Tom Kaczynski

ODOD Books
2854 Columbis Ave
Minneapolis, MN 55407
USA
ododbooks.com

ISBN: 978-1-941250-30-3

First Edition, August 2018

10 9 8 7 6 5 4 3 2 1

Printed in China

THat Night a MONSTER

Marzena Sowa

&

Berenika Kołomycka

ODOD
BOOKS

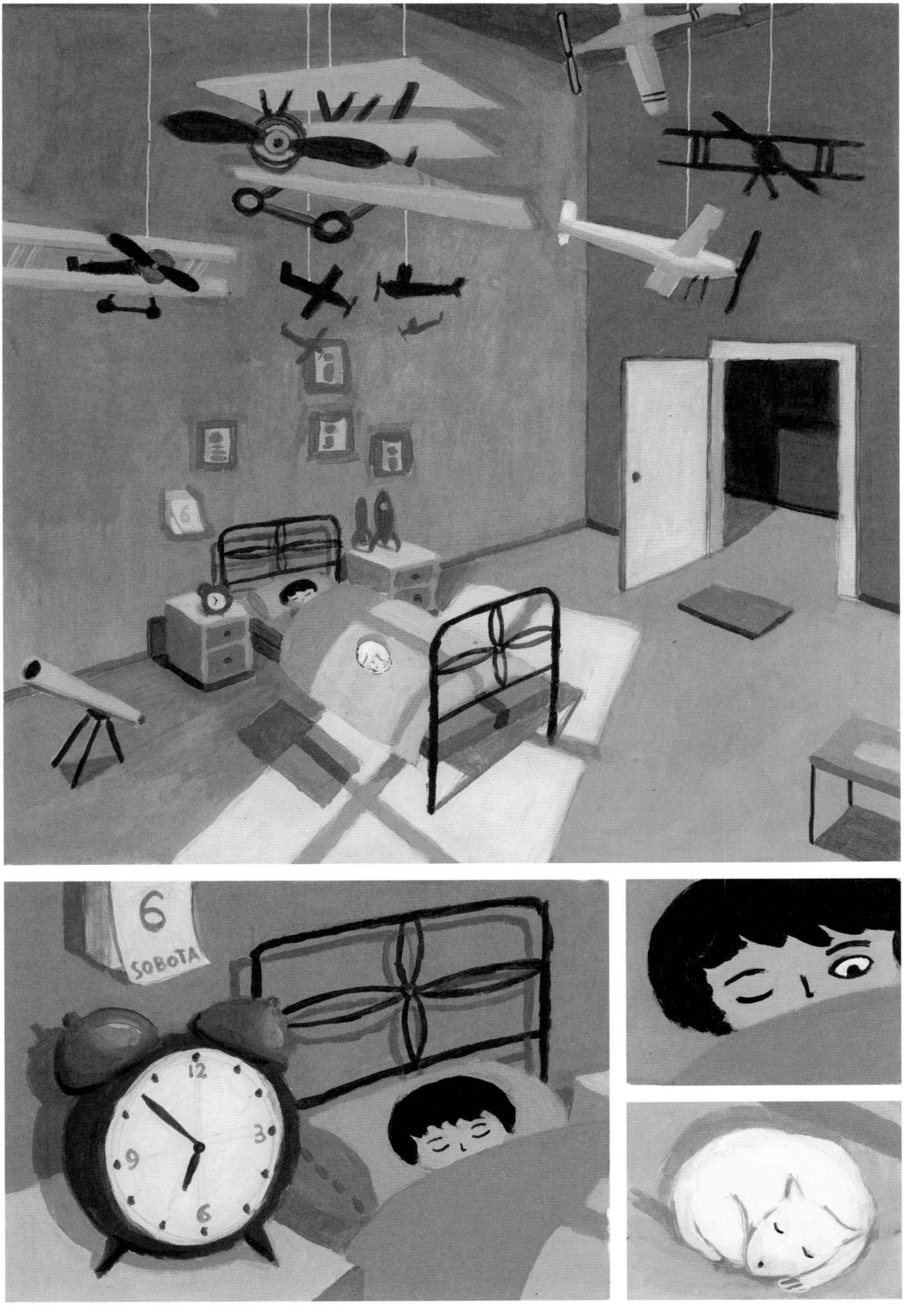
6
SOBOTA

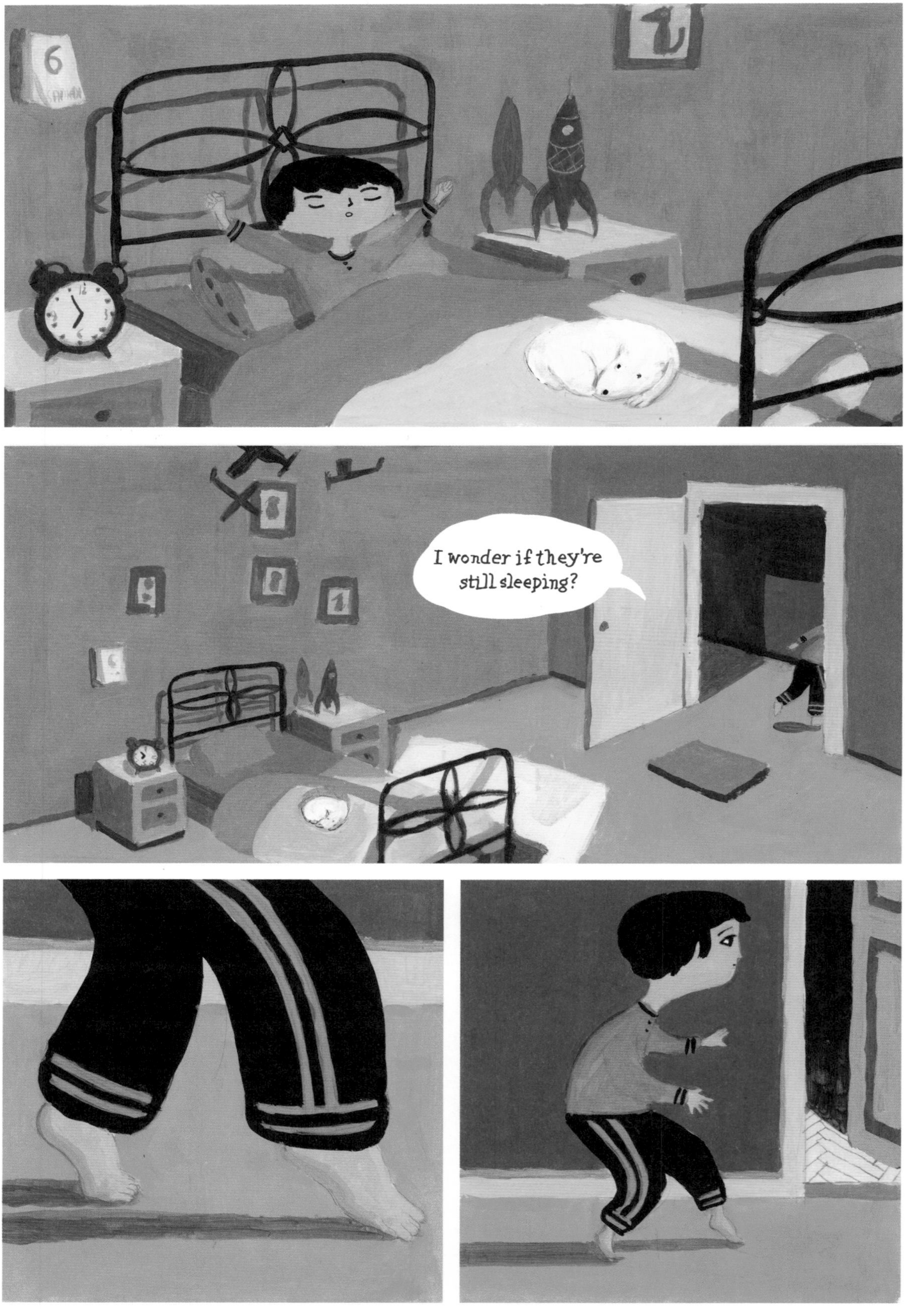
6
I wonder if they're still sleeping?

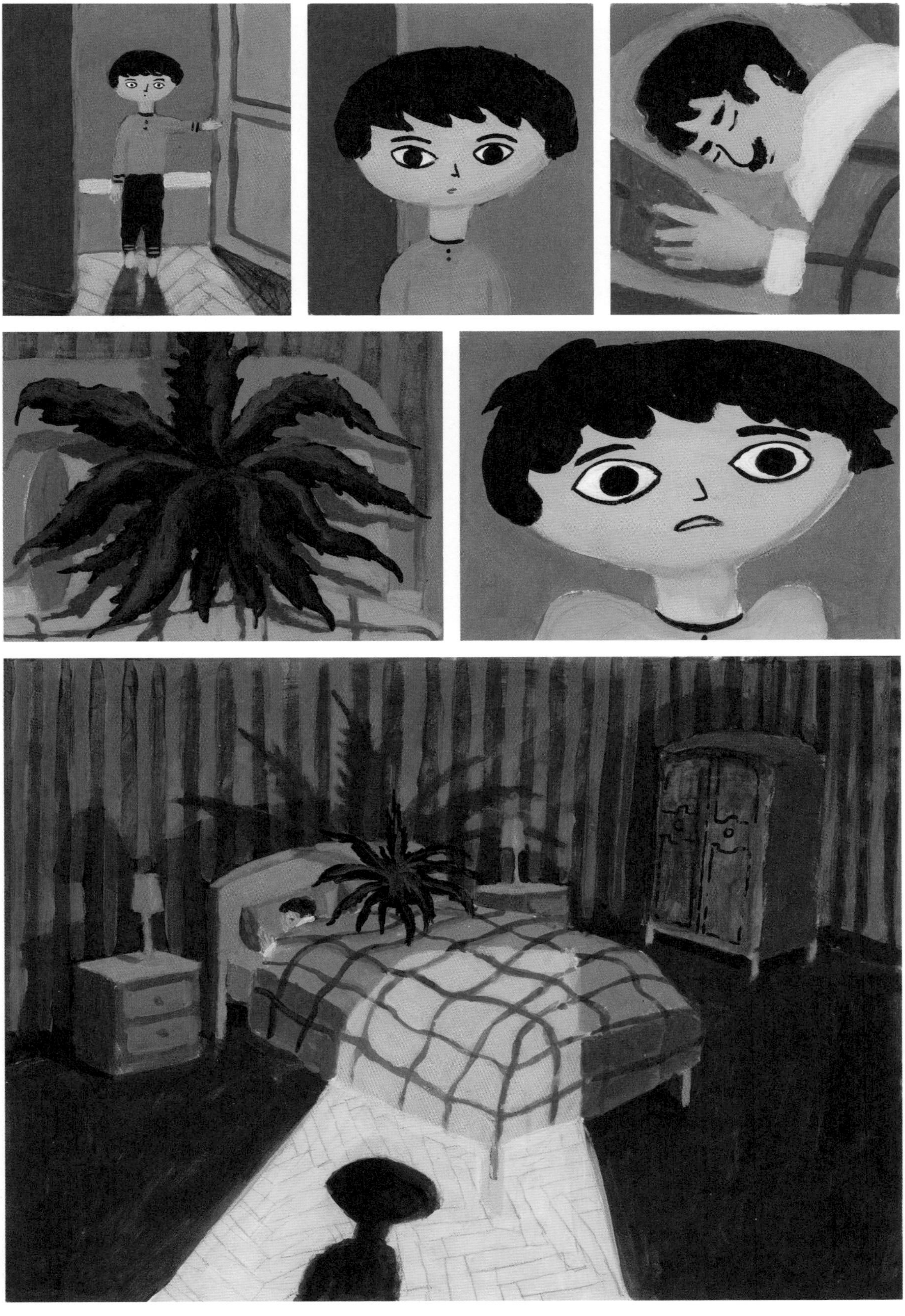

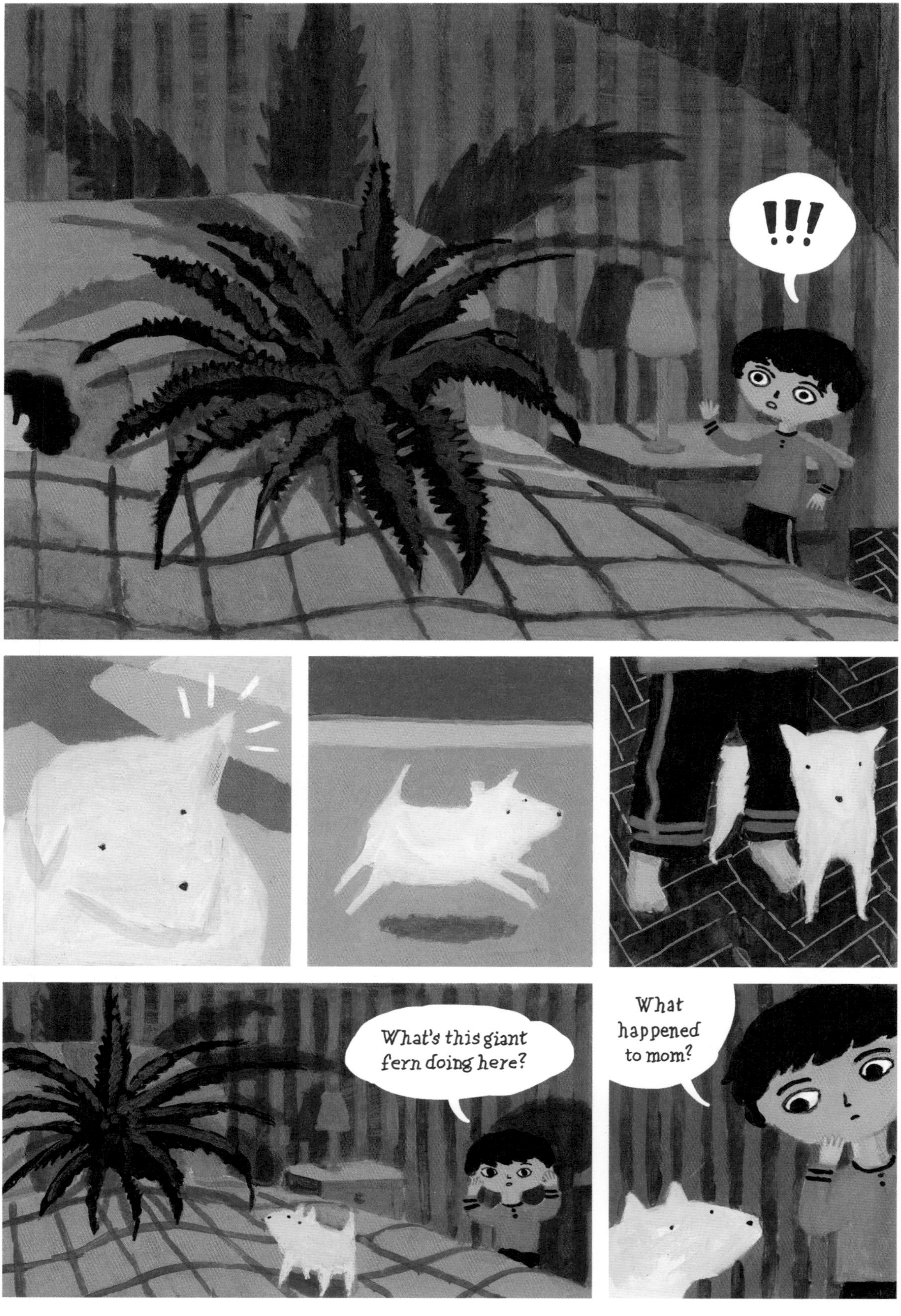
!!!
What's this giant fern doing here?
What happened to mom?

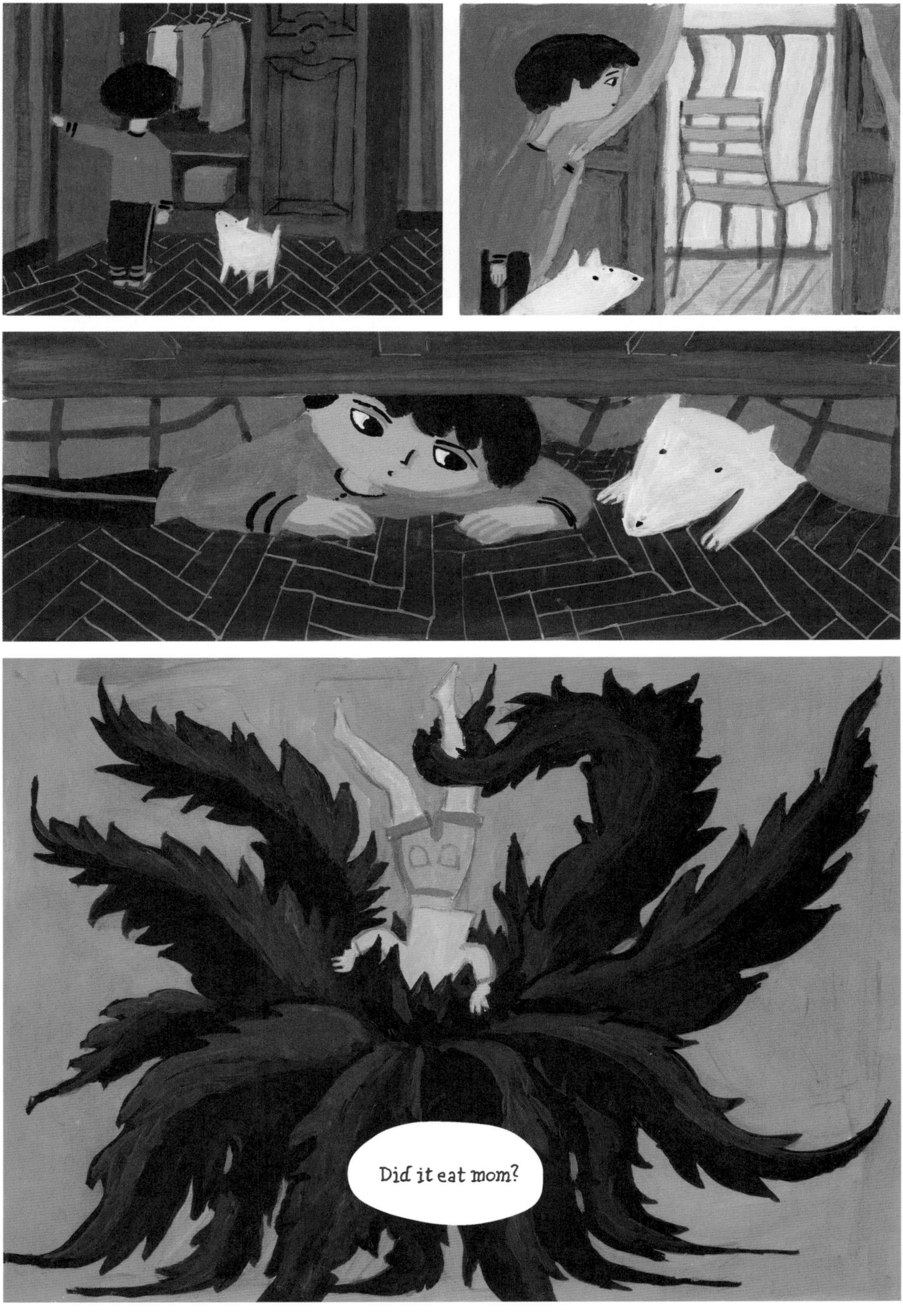
Did it eat mom?

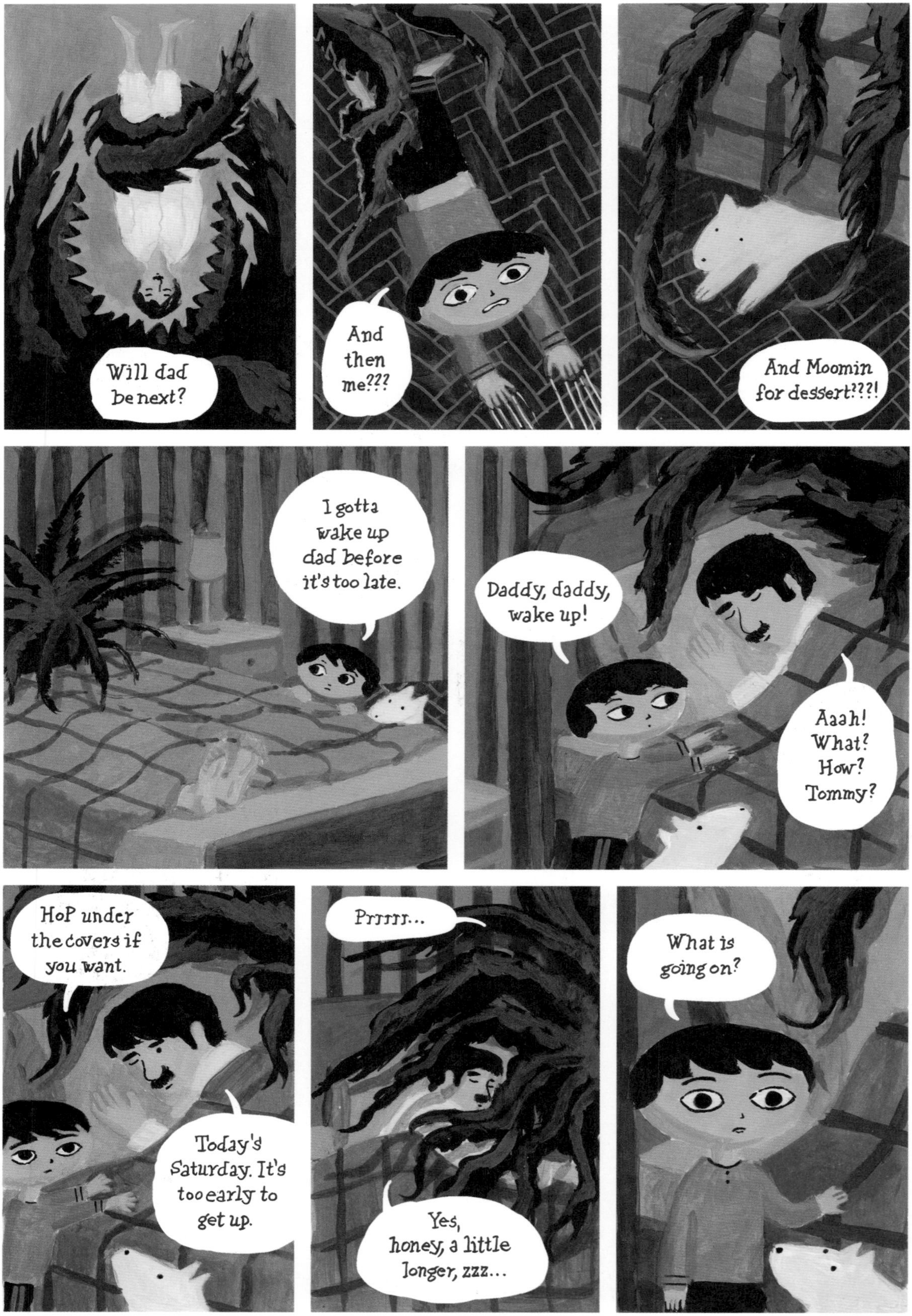
Will dad be next?
And then me???
And Moomin for dessert???!
I gotta wake up dad before it's too late.
Daddy, daddy, wake up!
Aaah! What? How? Tommy?
HoP under the covers if you want.
Today's Saturday. It's too early to get up.
Prrrrr...
Yes, honey, a little longer, zzz...
What is going on?

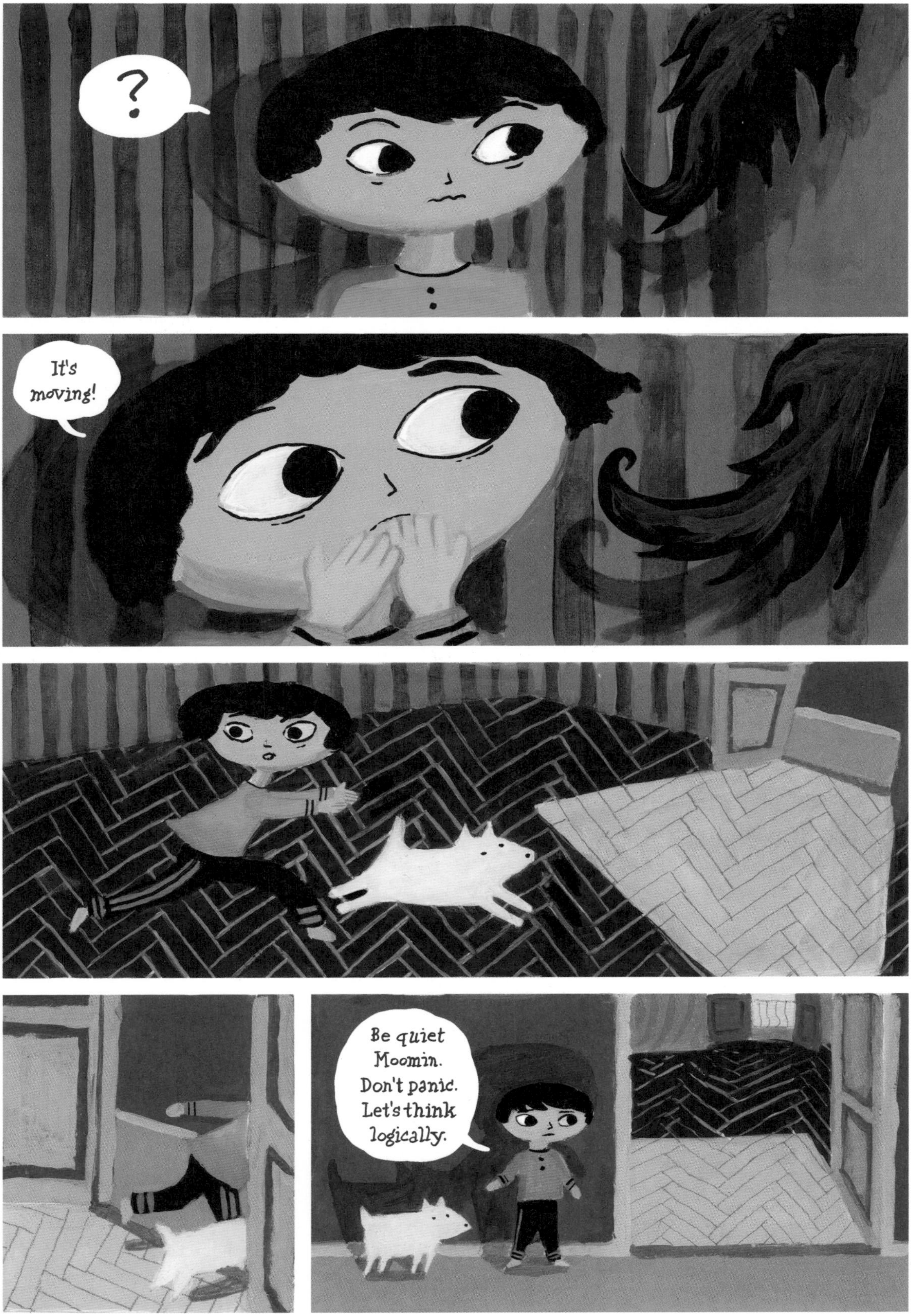
?
It's moving!
Be quiet Moomin. Don't panic. Let's think logically.

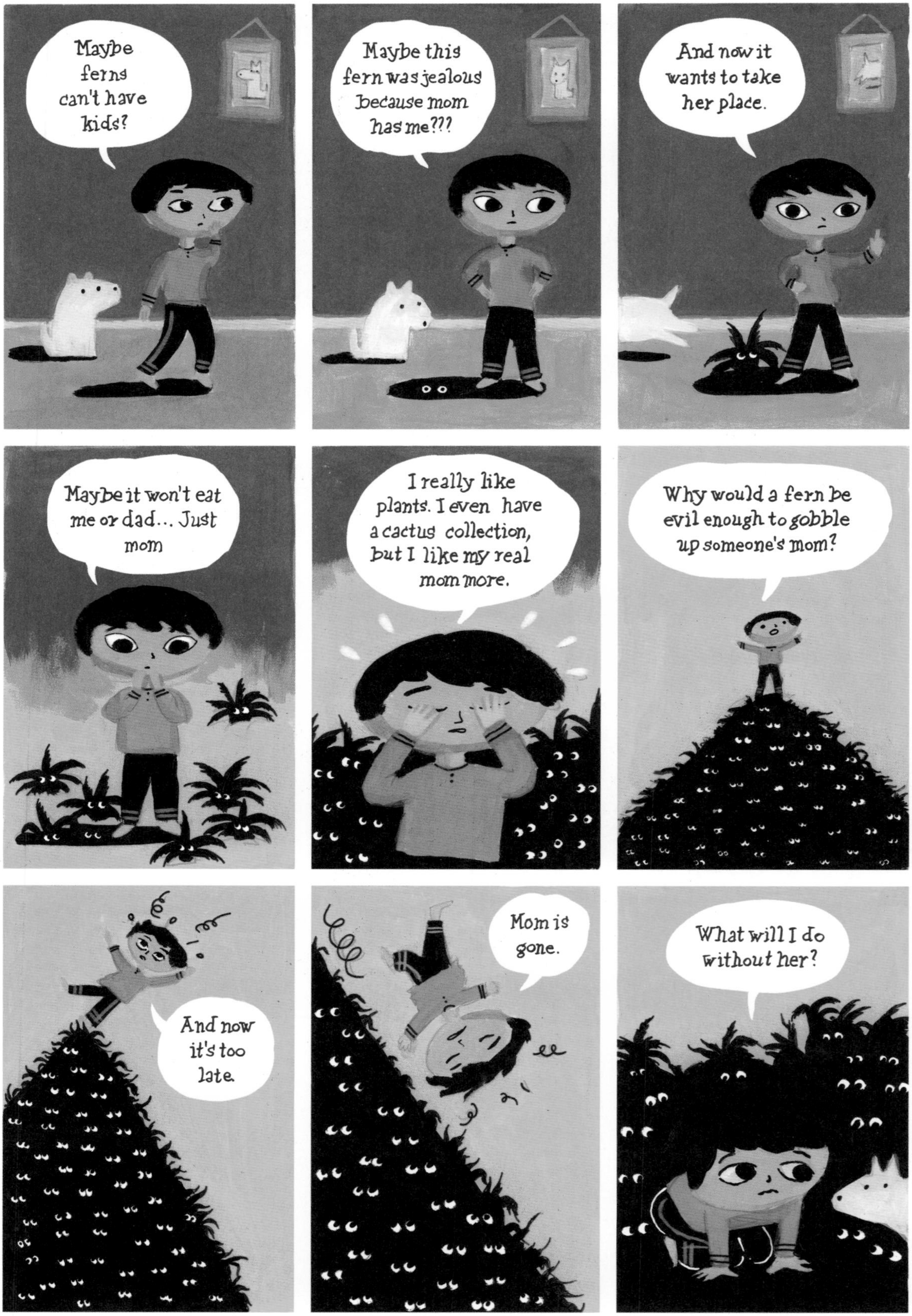

Maybe ferns can't have kids?
Maybe this fern was jealous because mom has me???
And now it wants to take her place.
Maybe it won't eat me or dad... Just mom
I really like plants. I even have a cactus collection, but I like my real mom more.
Why would a fern be evil enough to gobble up someone's mom?
And now it's too late.
Mom is gone.
What will I do without her?

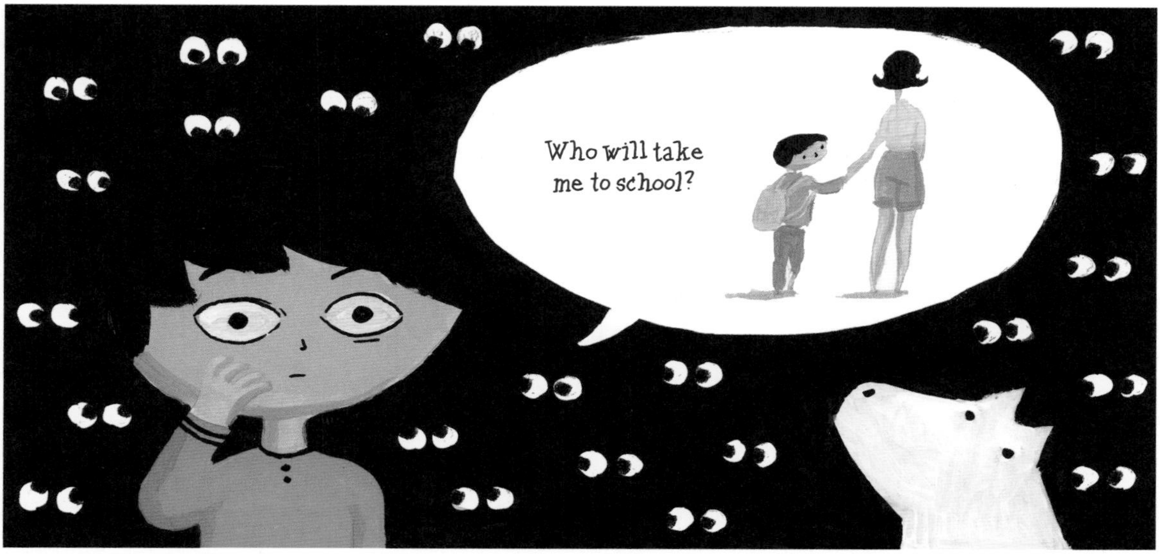
Who will take me to school?

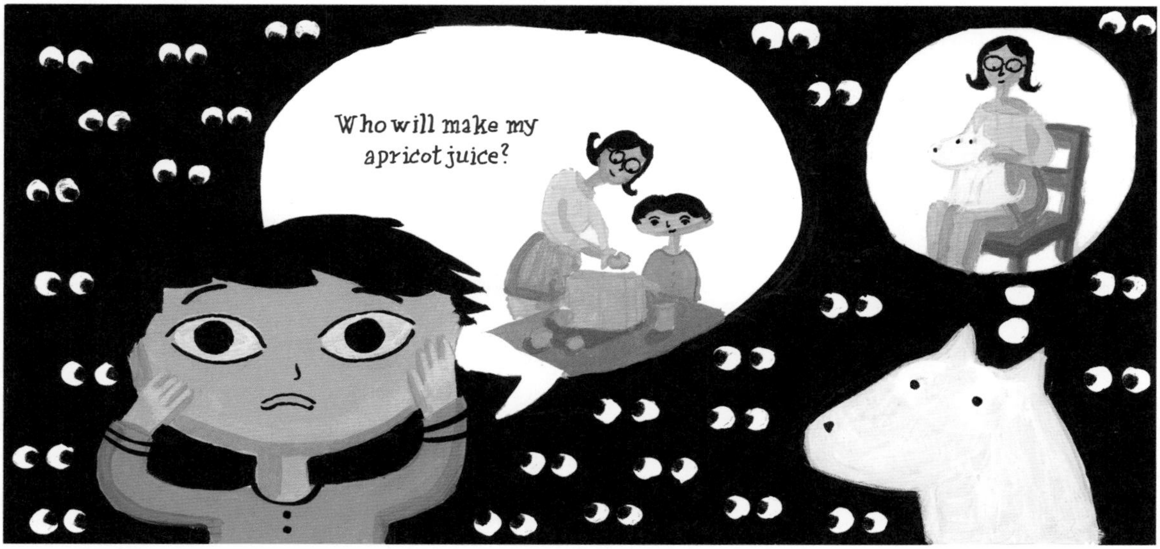
Who will make my apricot juice?

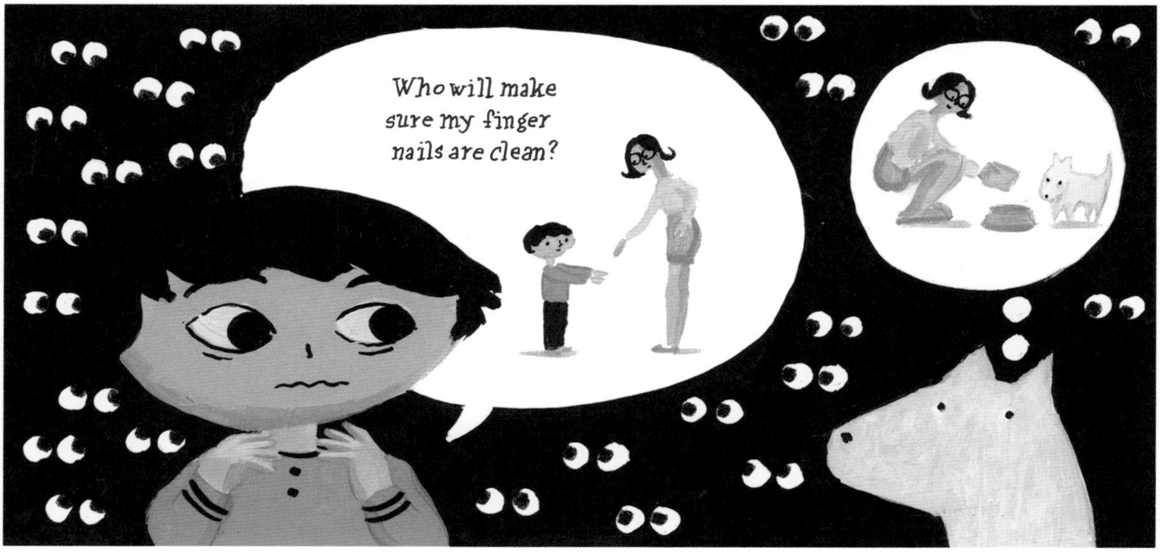
Who will make sure my finger nails are clean?

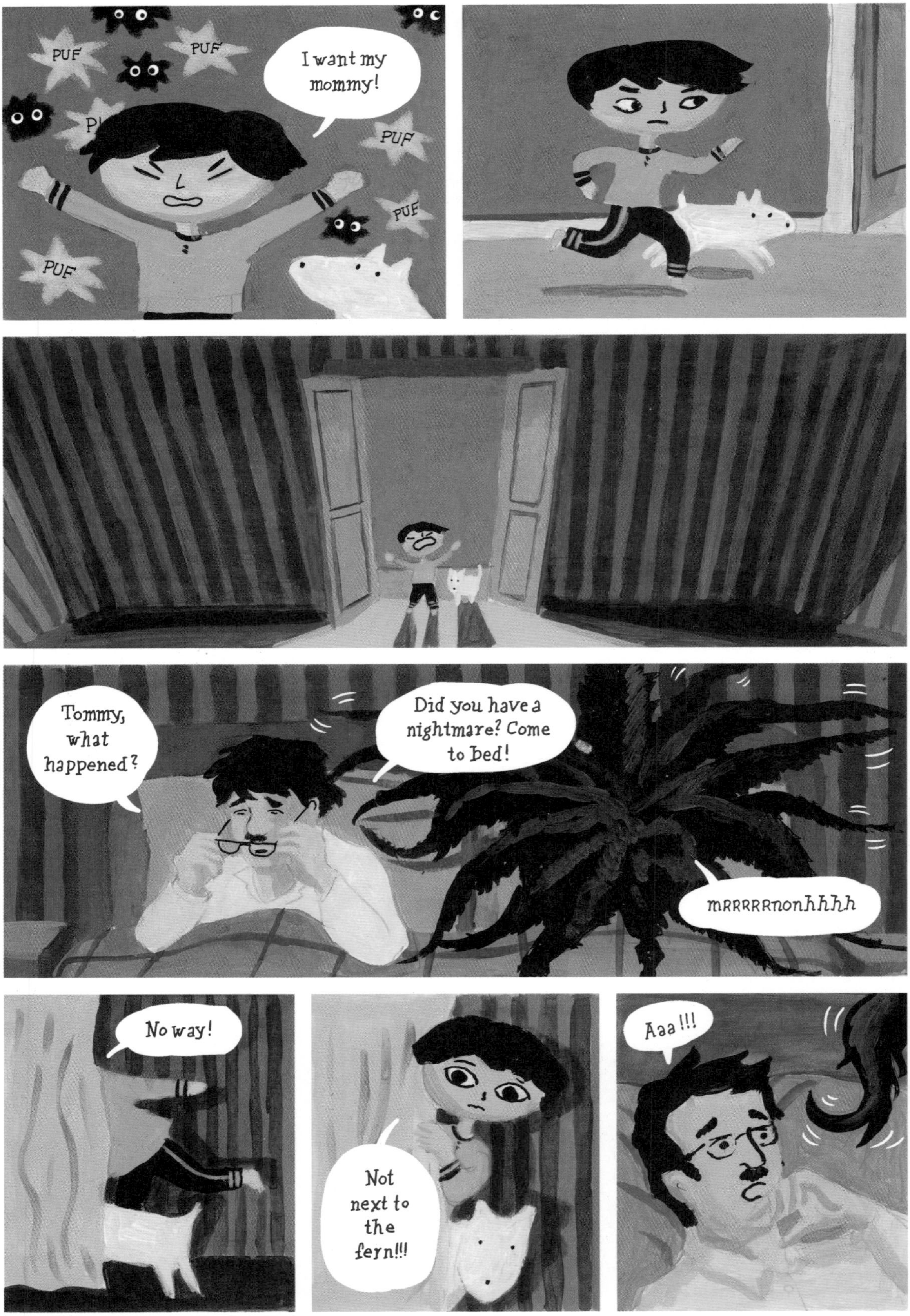
PUF
PUF
I want my mommy!
PUF
PUF
PUF
Tommy, what happened?
Did you have a nightmare? Come to bed!
mrrrrrnonhhhh
No way!
Not next to the fern!!!
Aaa!!!

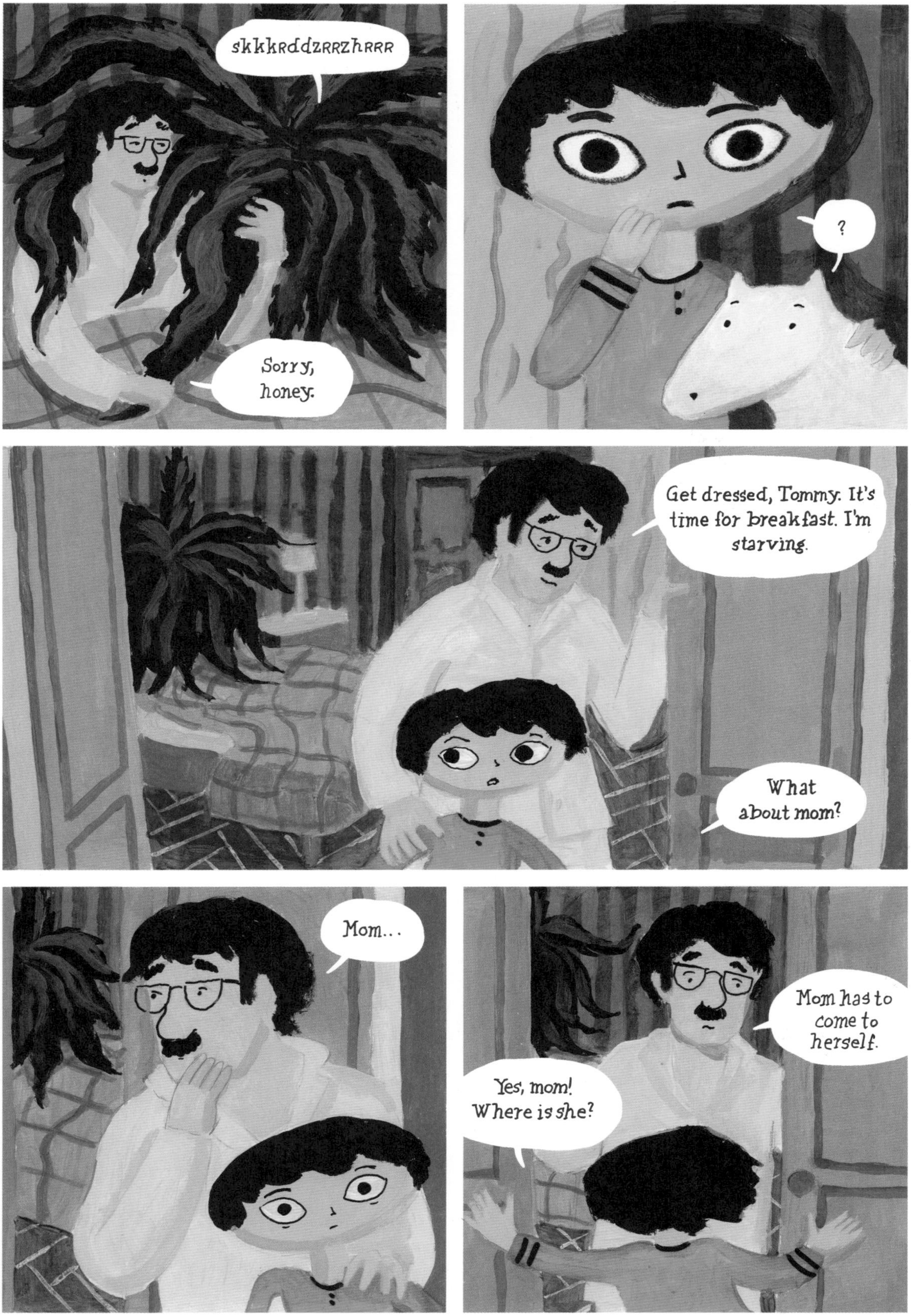
skkkrddzrrzhrrr
Sorry, honey.
?
Get dressed, Tommy. It's time for breakfast. I'm starving.
What about mom?
Mom...
Mom has to come to herself.
Yes, mom! Where is she?

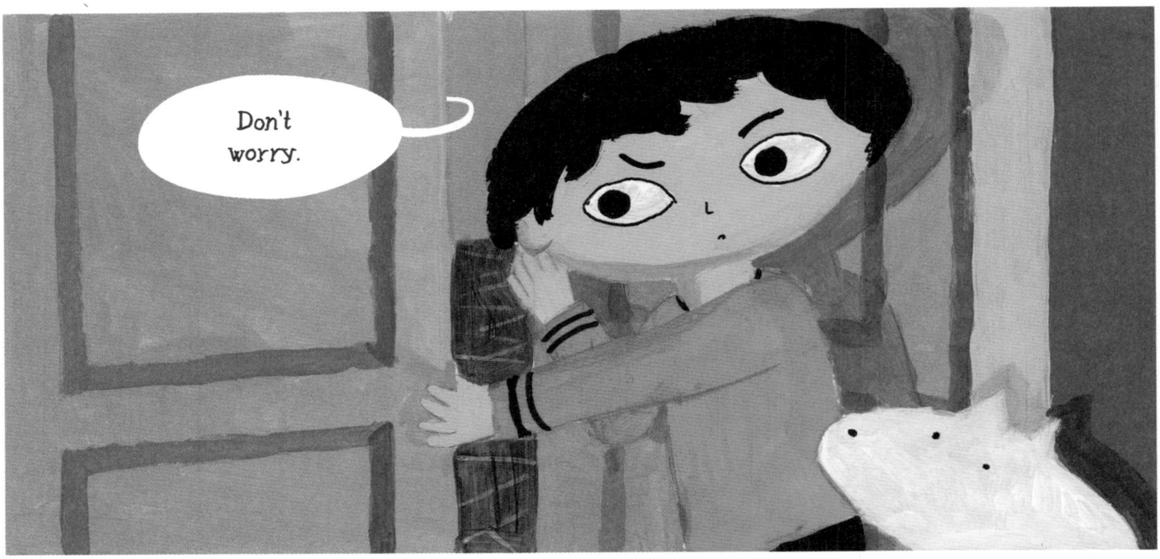
Don't worry.

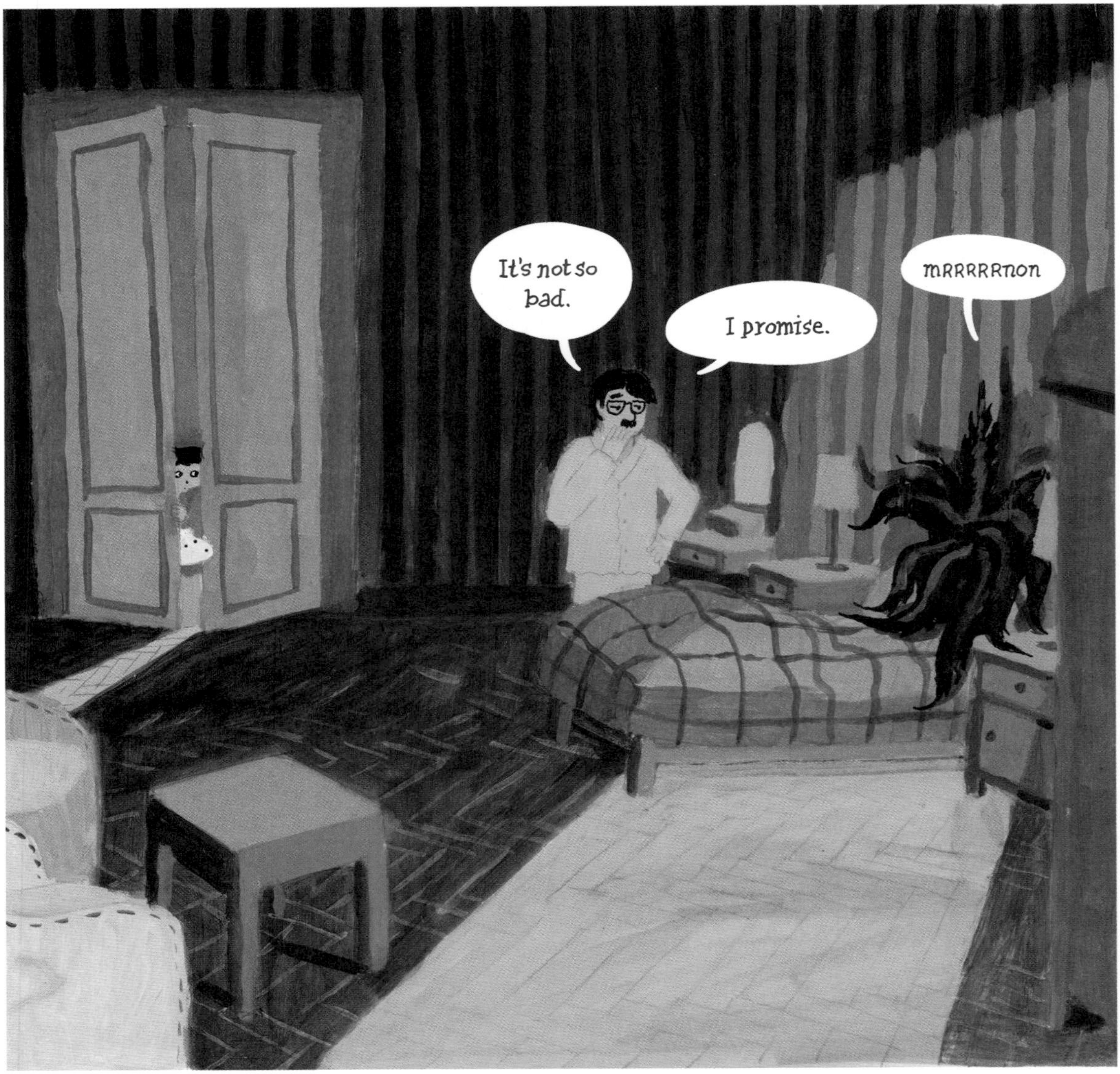
It's not so bad.
I promise.
mrrrrrnon

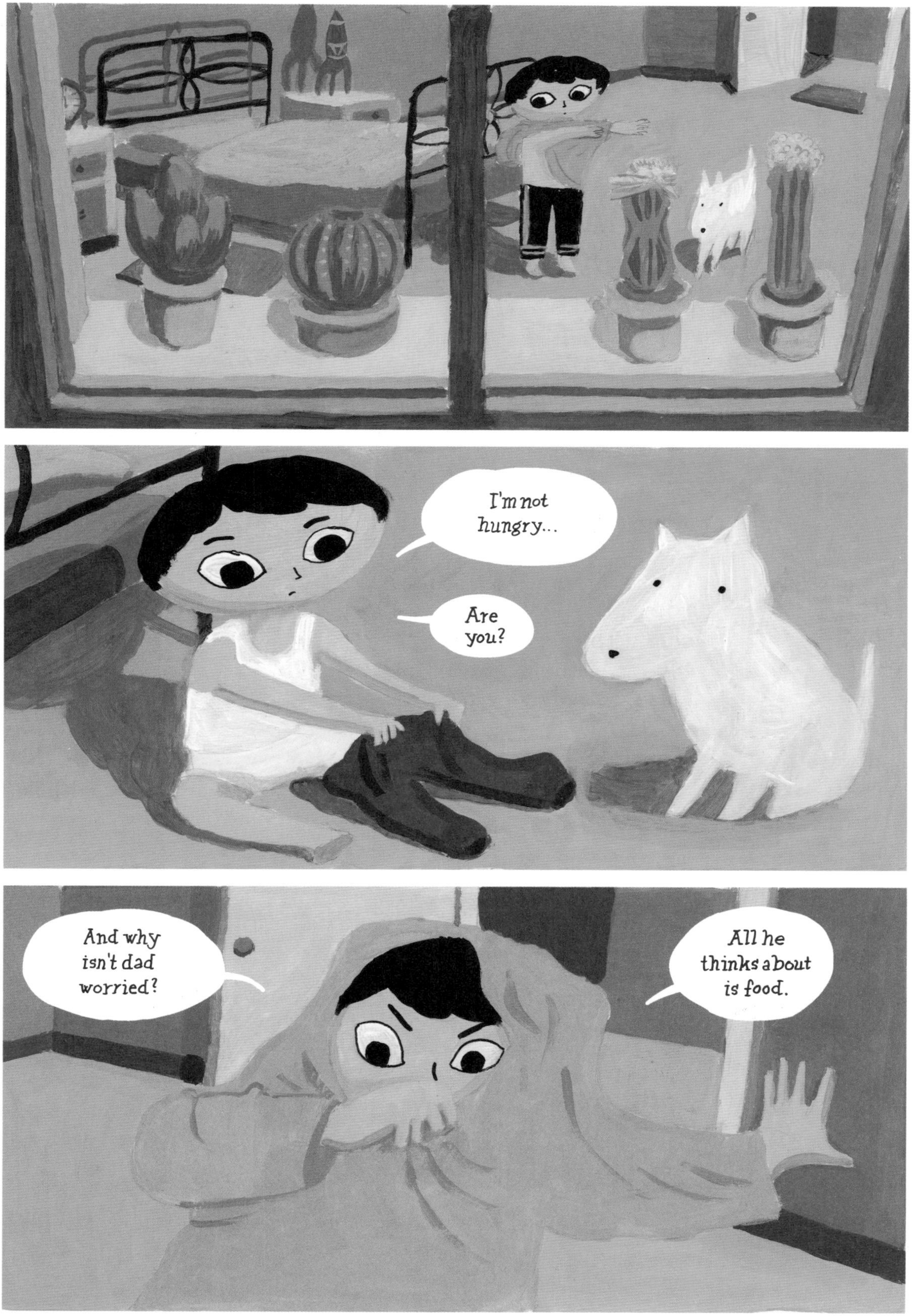

I'm not hungry...
Are you?
And why isn't dad worried?
All he thinks about is food.

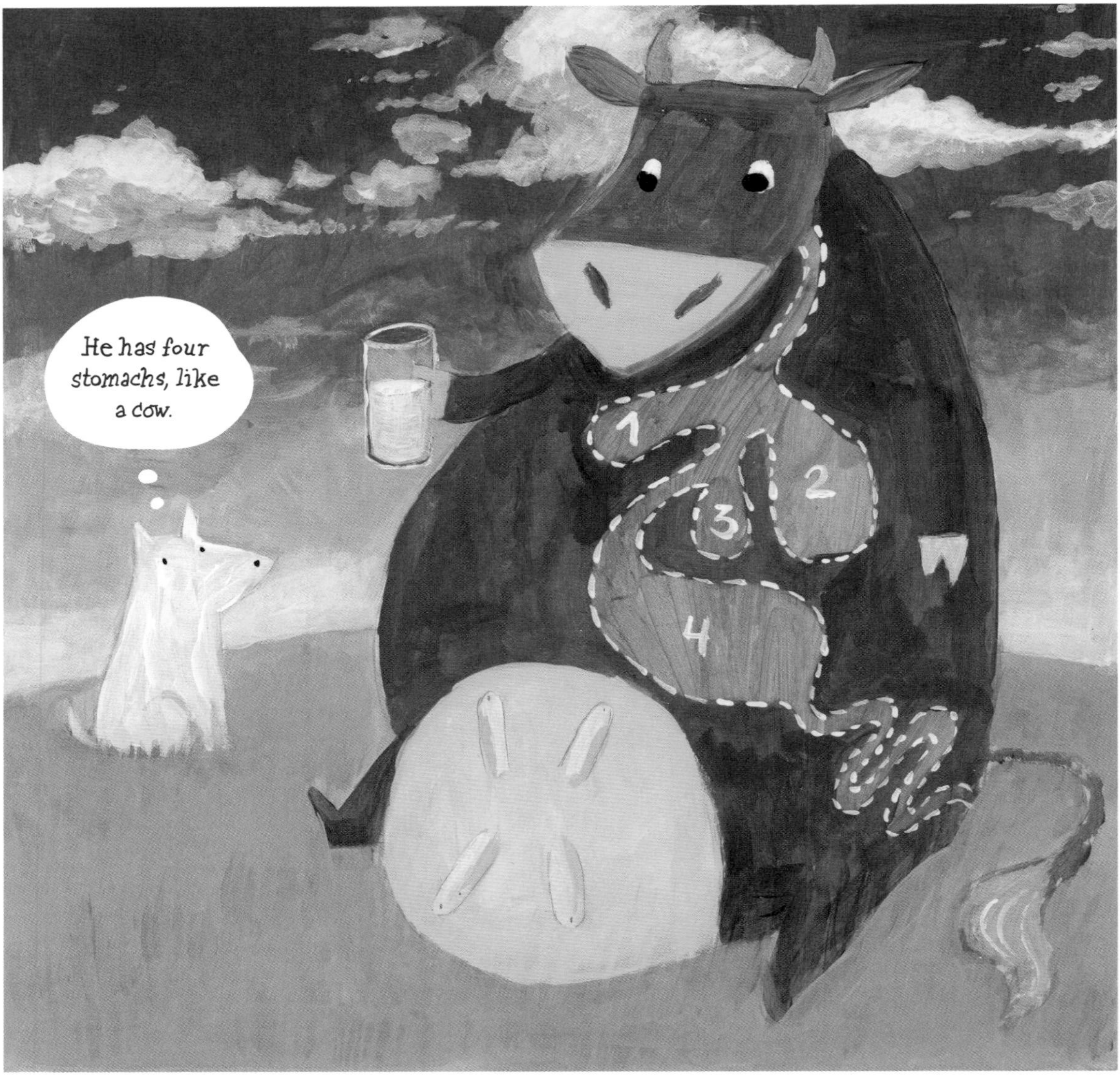
He has four stomachs, like a cow.
1
2
3
4

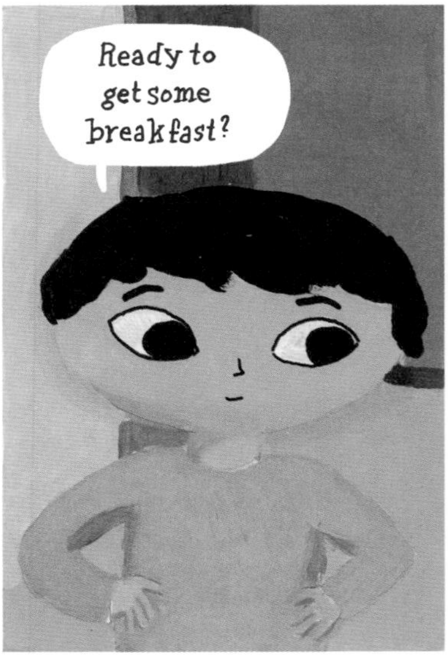
Ready to get some breakfast?

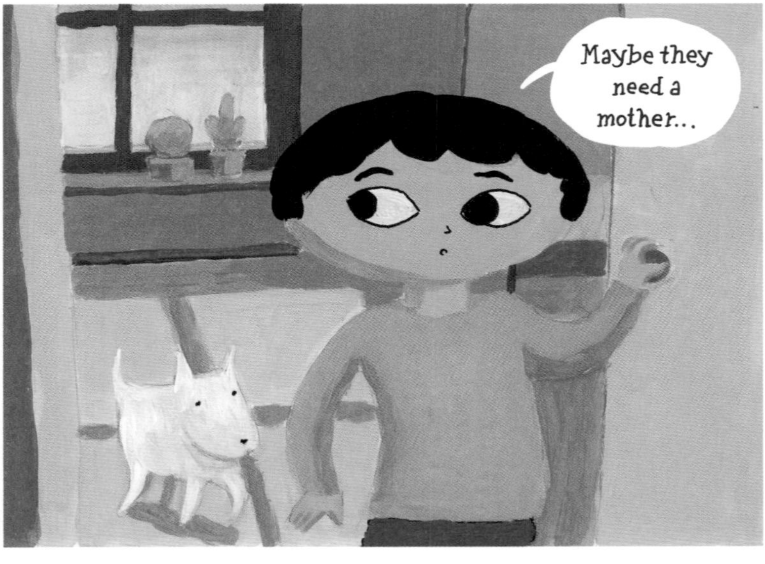
Maybe they need a mother...

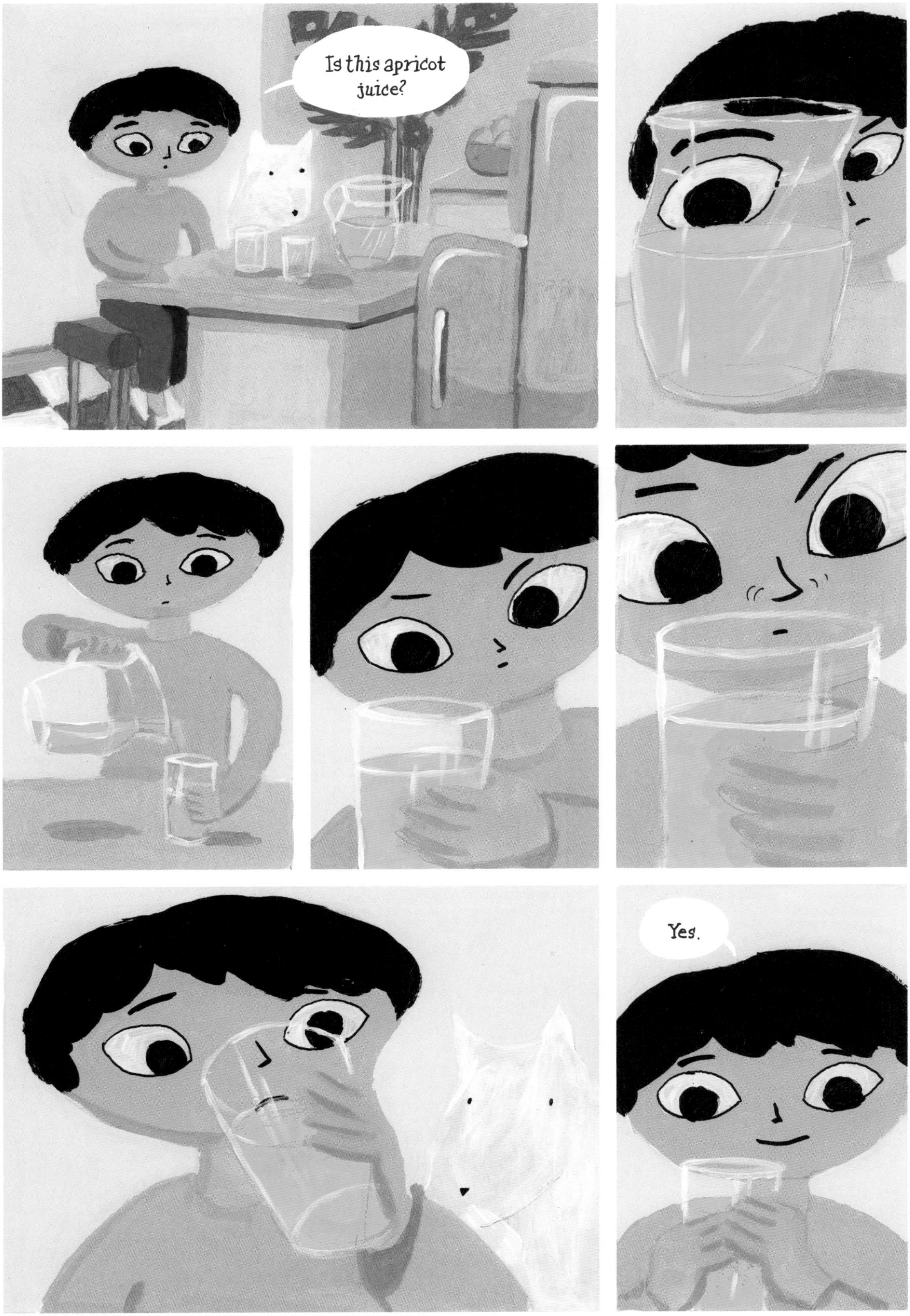
Is this apricot juice?
Yes.

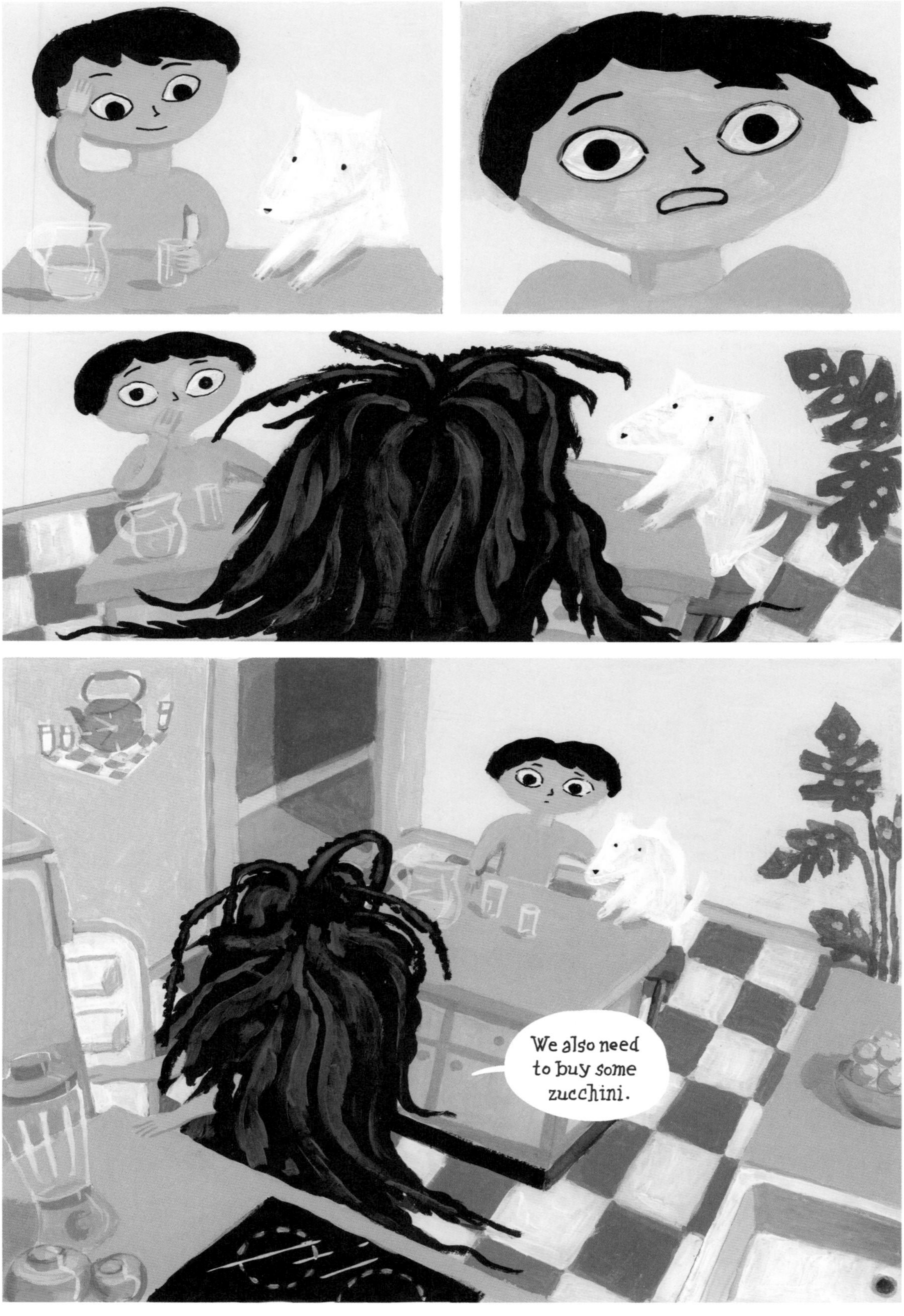
We also need to buy some zucchini.

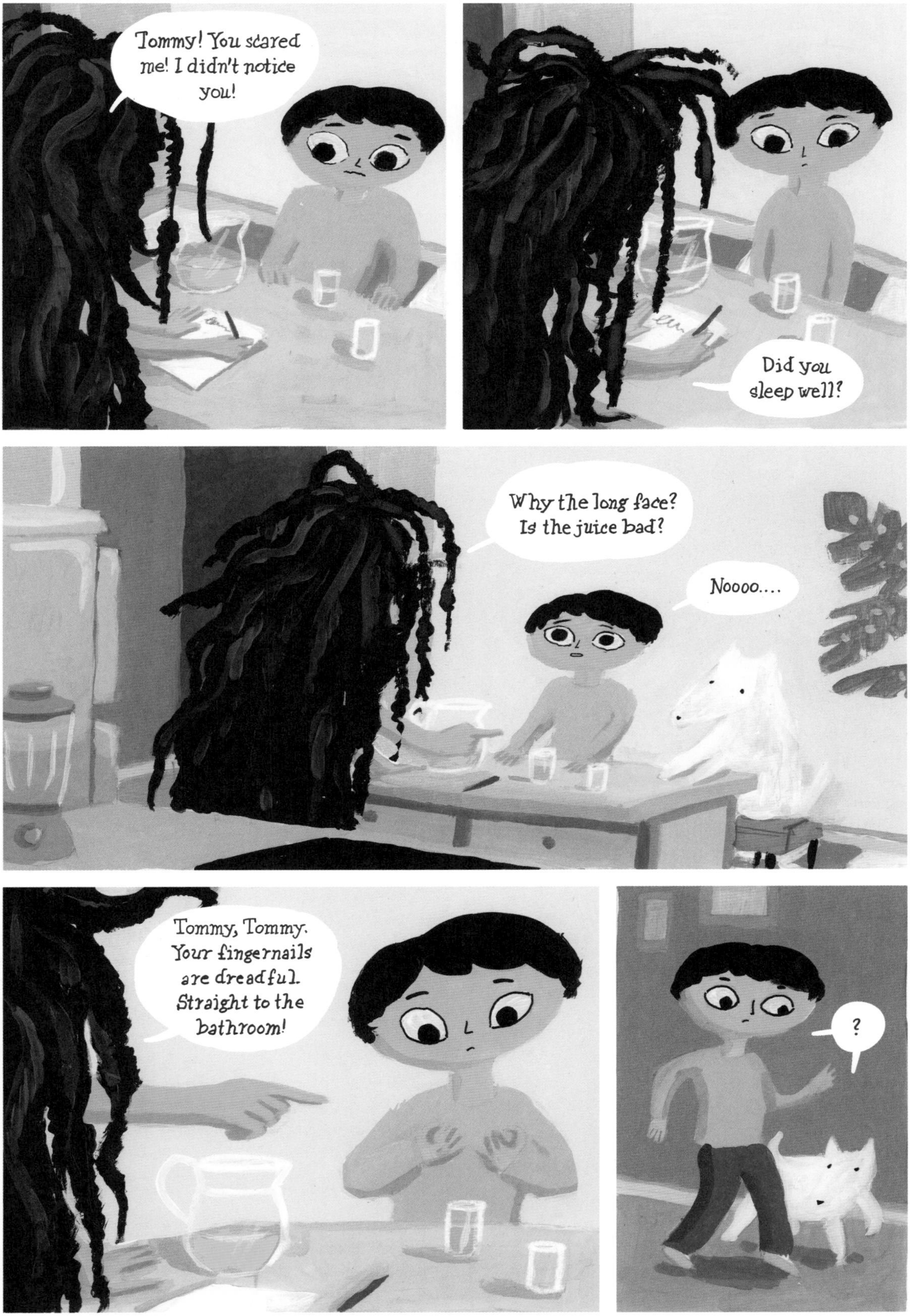

Tommy! You scared me! I didn't notice you!
Did you sleep well?
Why the long face? Is the juice bad?
Noooo....
Tommy, Tommy. Your fingernails are dreadful. Straight to the bathroom!
?

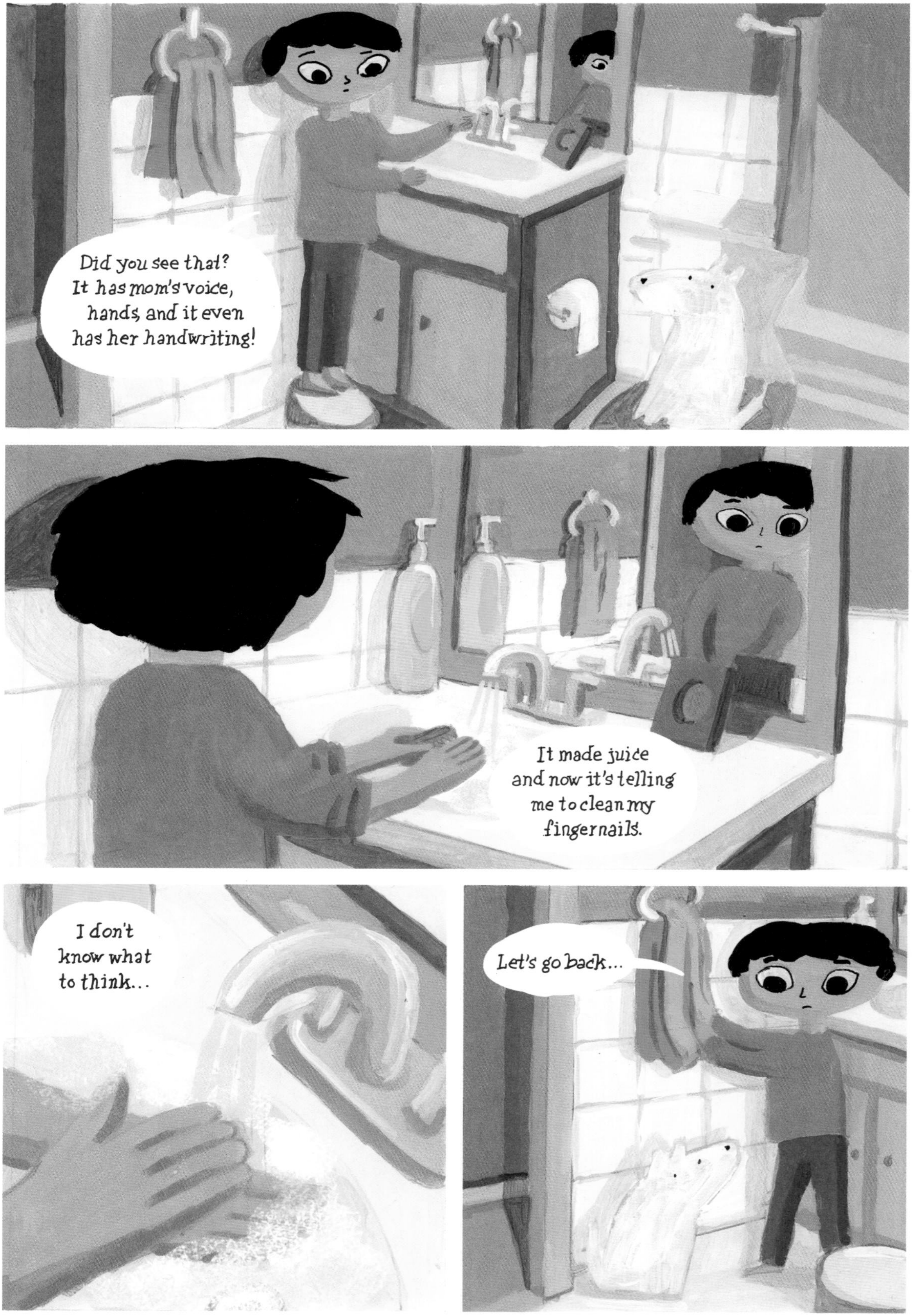
Did you see that? It has mom's voice, hands, and it even has her handwriting!
It made juice and now it's telling me to clean my fingernails.
I don't know what to think...
Let's go back...

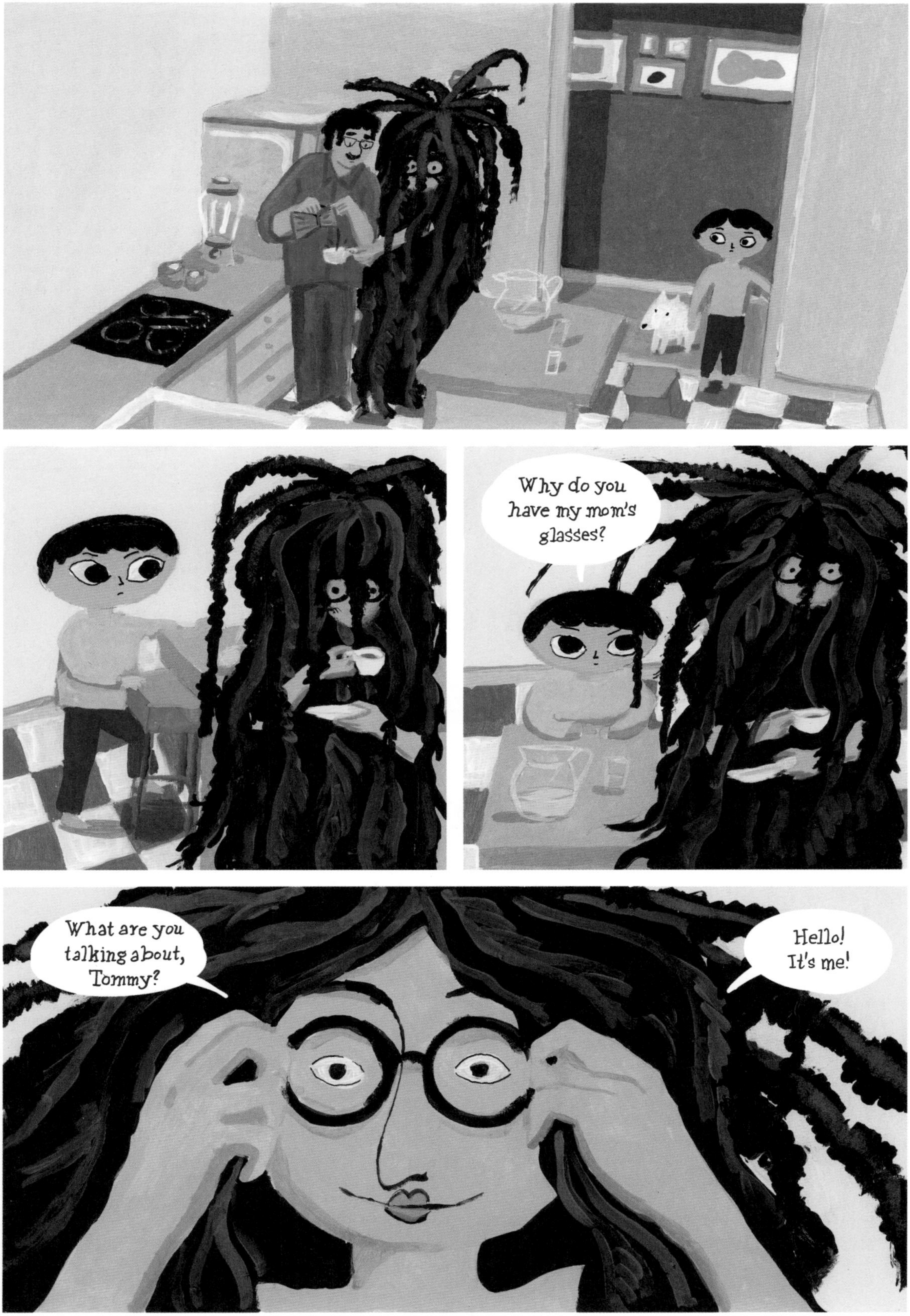
Why do you have my mom's glasses?
What are you talking about, Tommy?
Hello! It's me!

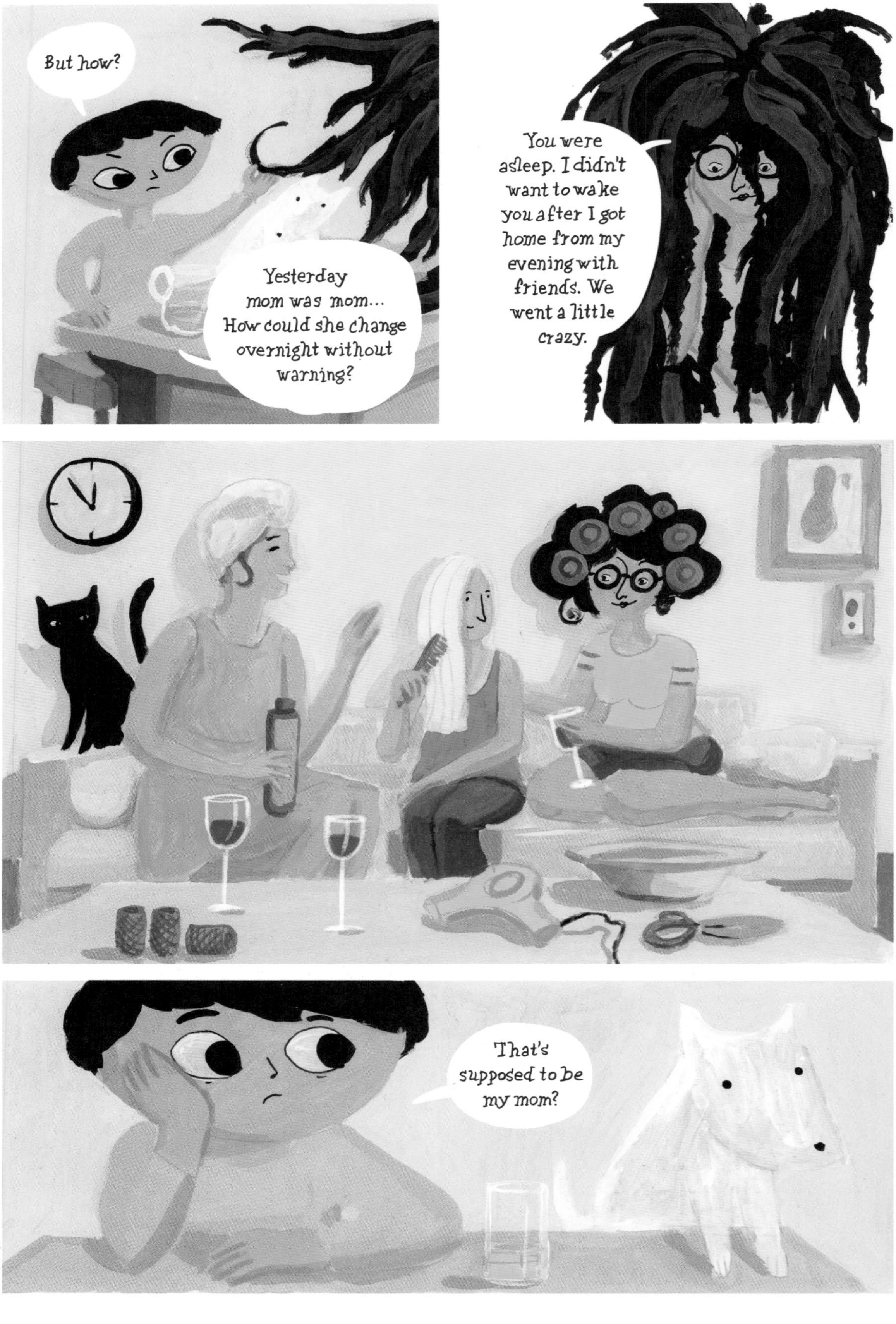
But how?
Yesterday mom was mom... How could she change overnight without warning?
You were asleep. I didn't want to wake you after I got home from my evening with friends. We went a little crazy.
That's supposed to be my mom?

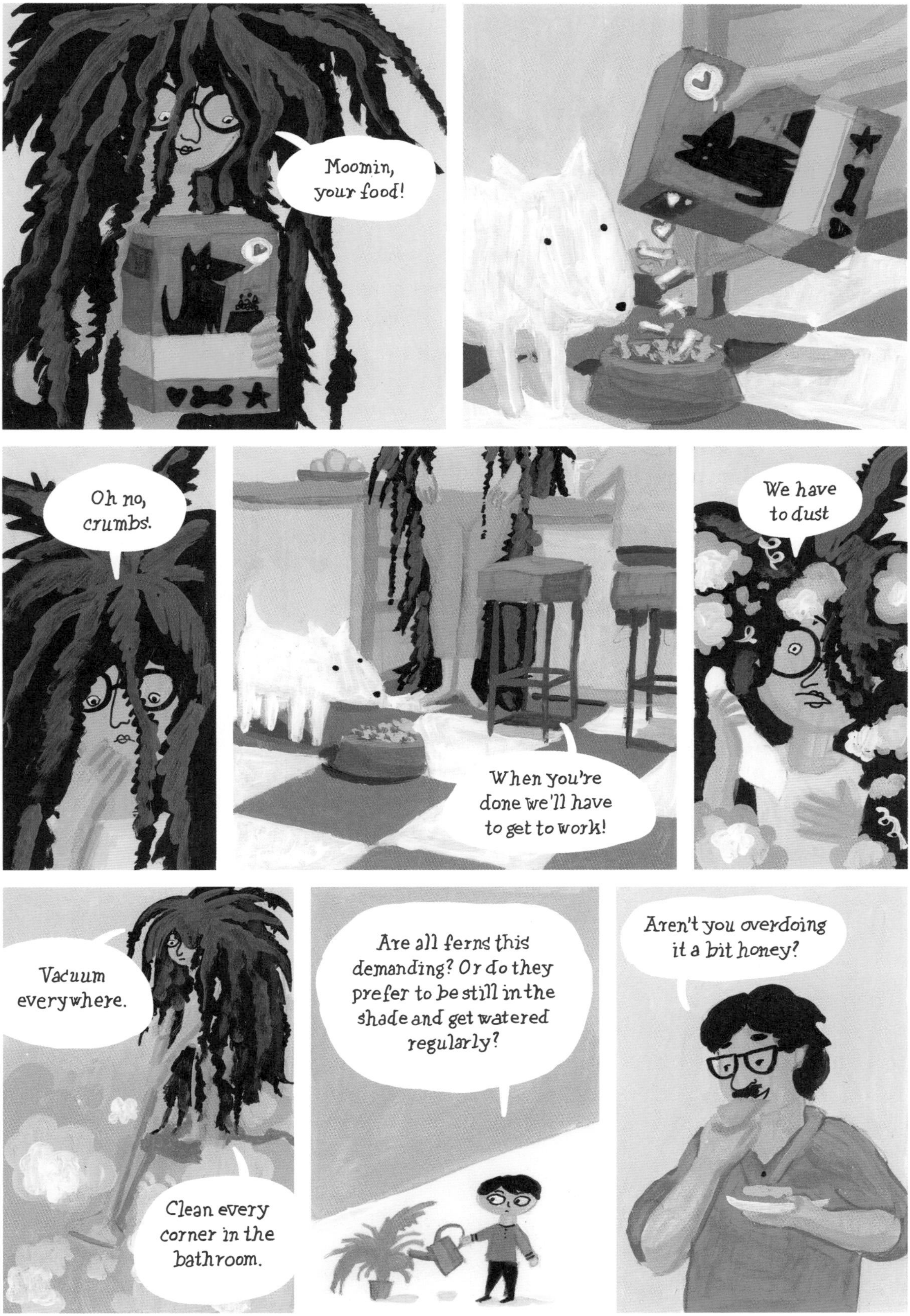

Moomin, your food!
Oh no, crumbs.
When you're done we'll have to get to work!
We have to dust
Vacuum everywhere.
Clean every corner in the bathroom.
Are all ferns this demanding? Or do they prefer to be still in the shade and get watered regularly?
Aren't you overdoing it a bit honey?

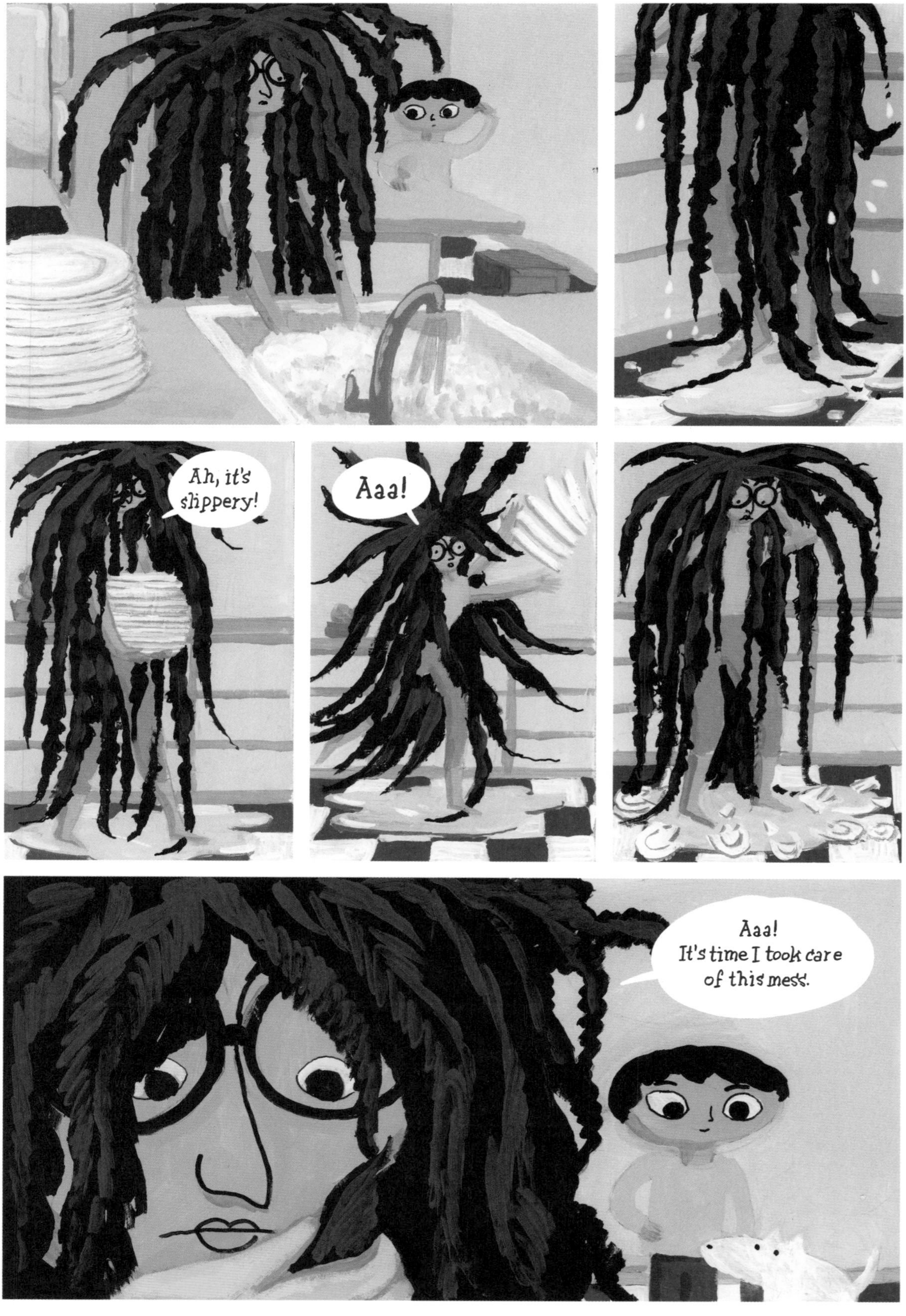
Ah, it's slippery!
Aaa!
Aaa! It's time I took care of this mess!

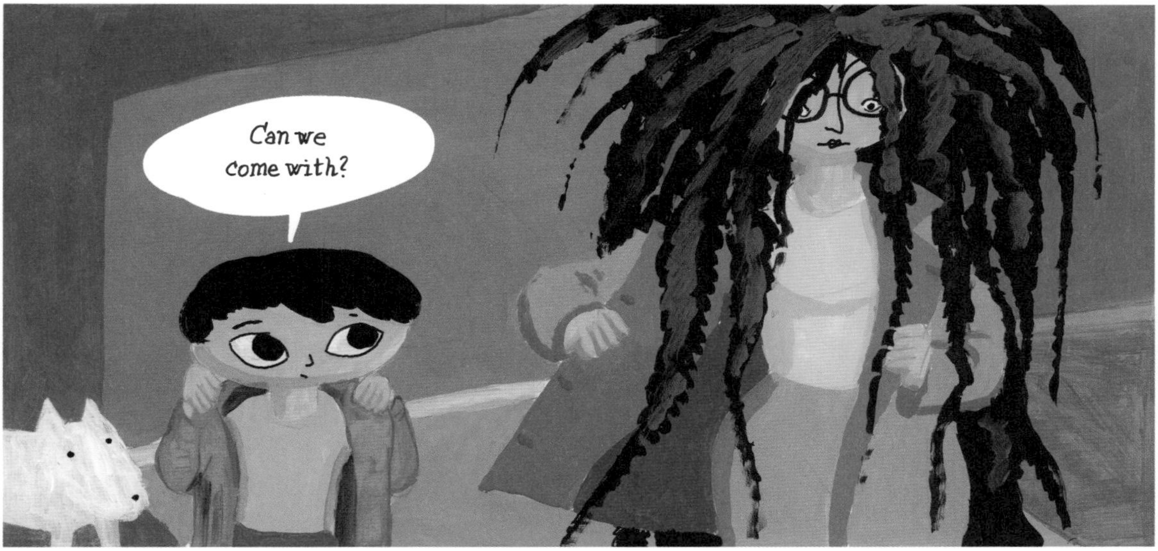
Can we come with?

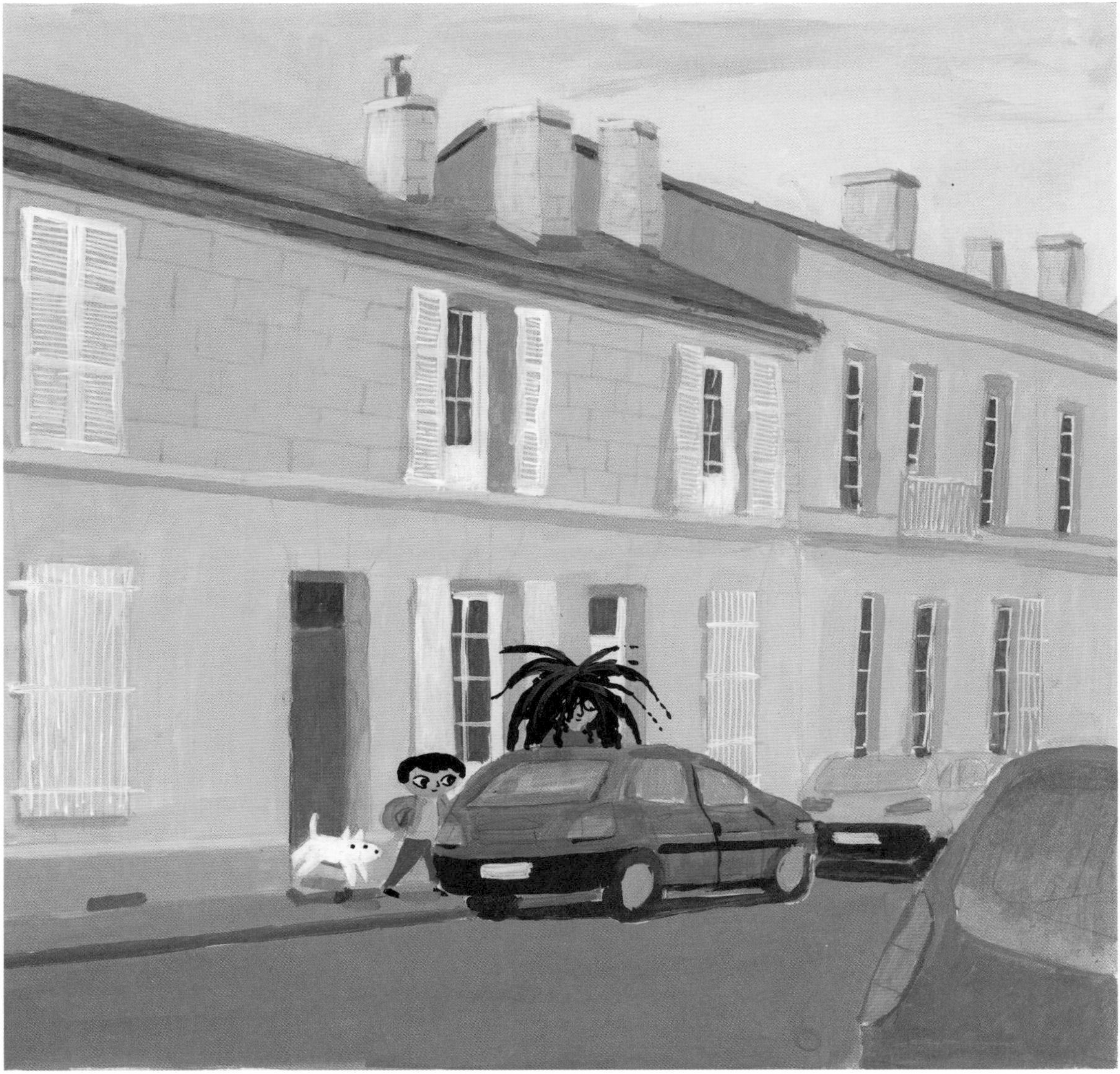

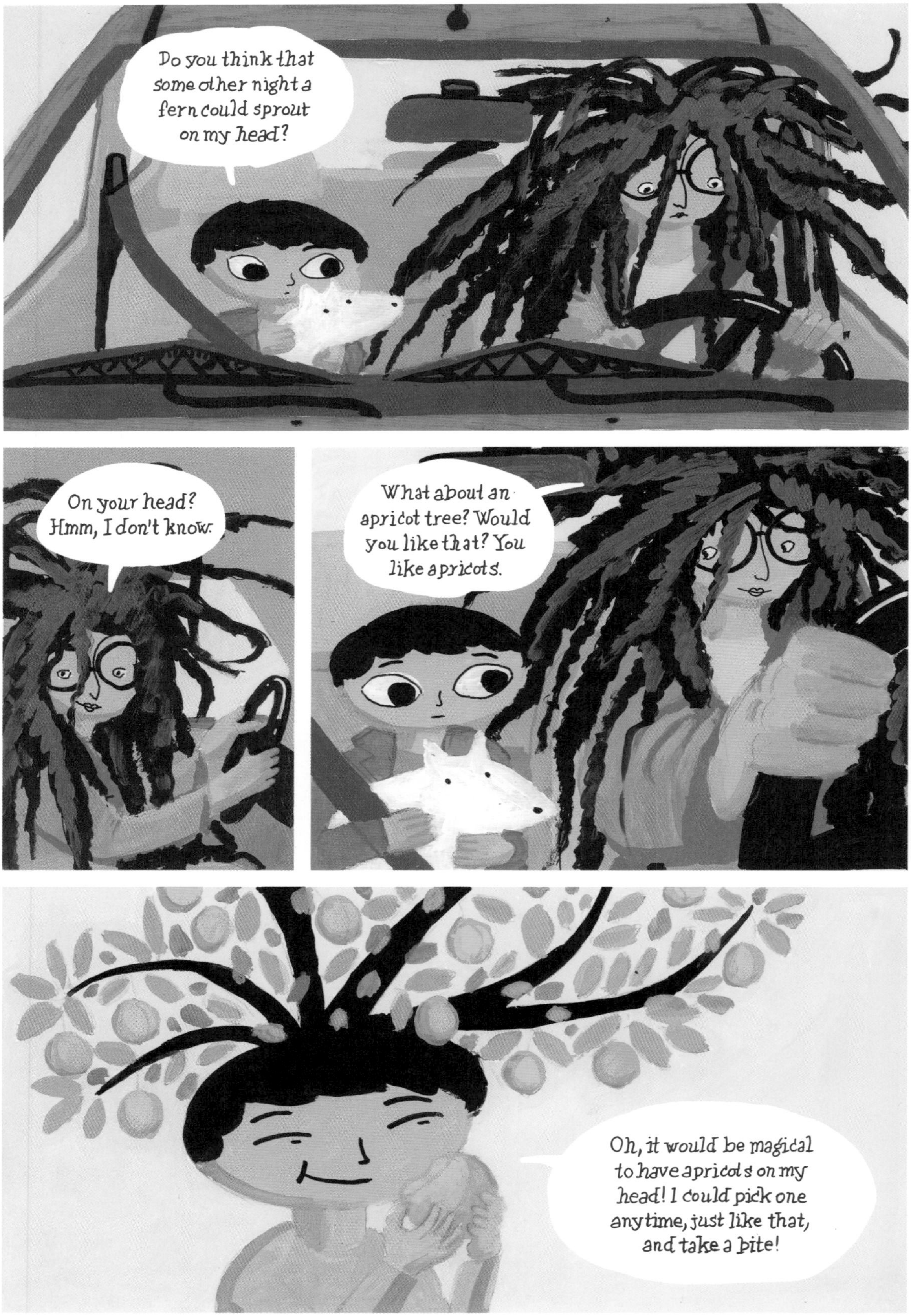
Do you think that some other night a fern could sprout on my head?
On your head? Hmm, I don't know.
What about an apricot tree? Would you like that? You like apricots.
Oh, it would be magical to have apricots on my head! I could pick one anytime, just like that, and take a bite!

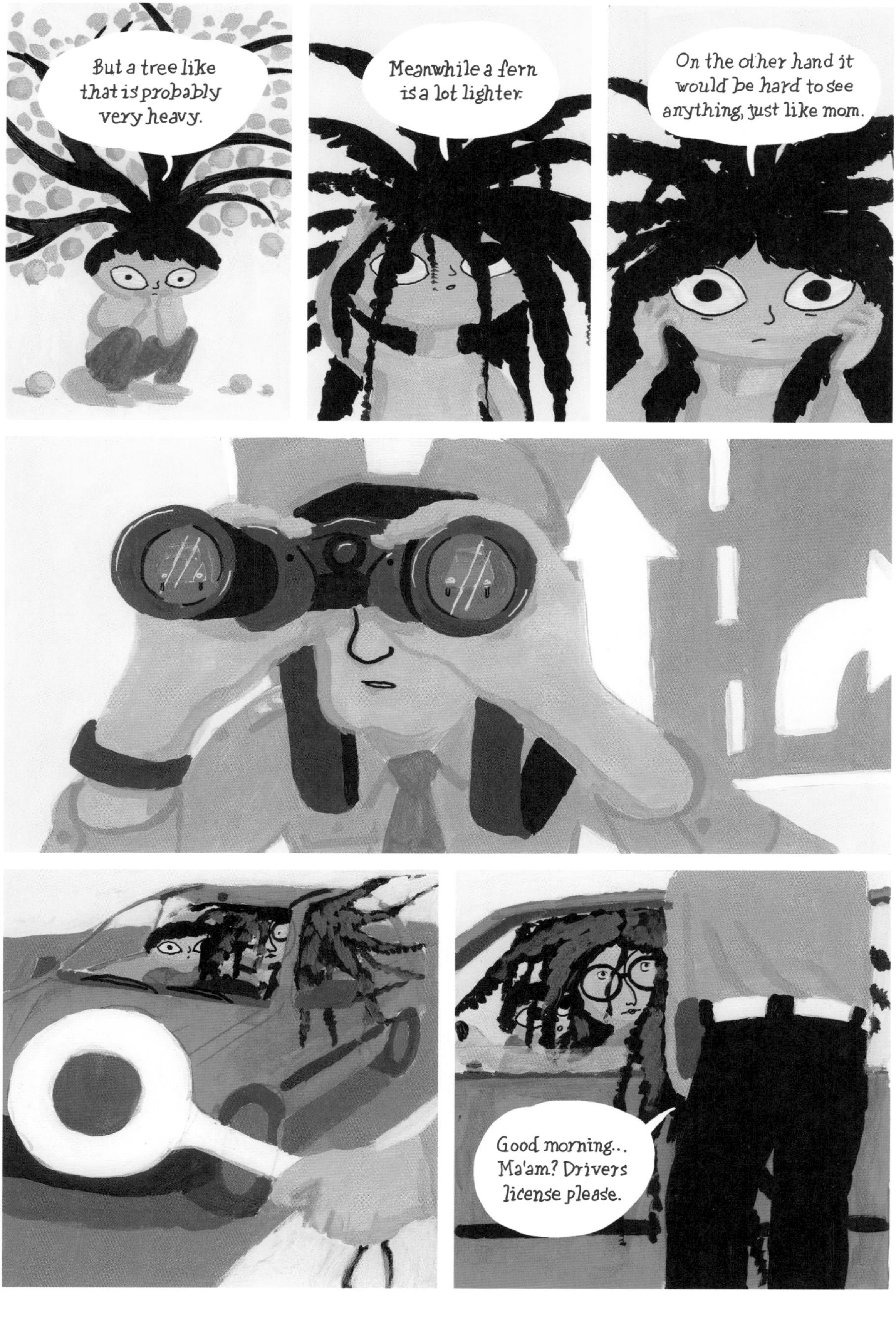
But a tree like that is probably very heavy.
Meanwhile a fern is a lot lighter.
On the other hand it would be hard to see anything, just like mom.
Good morning.. Ma'am? Drivers license please.

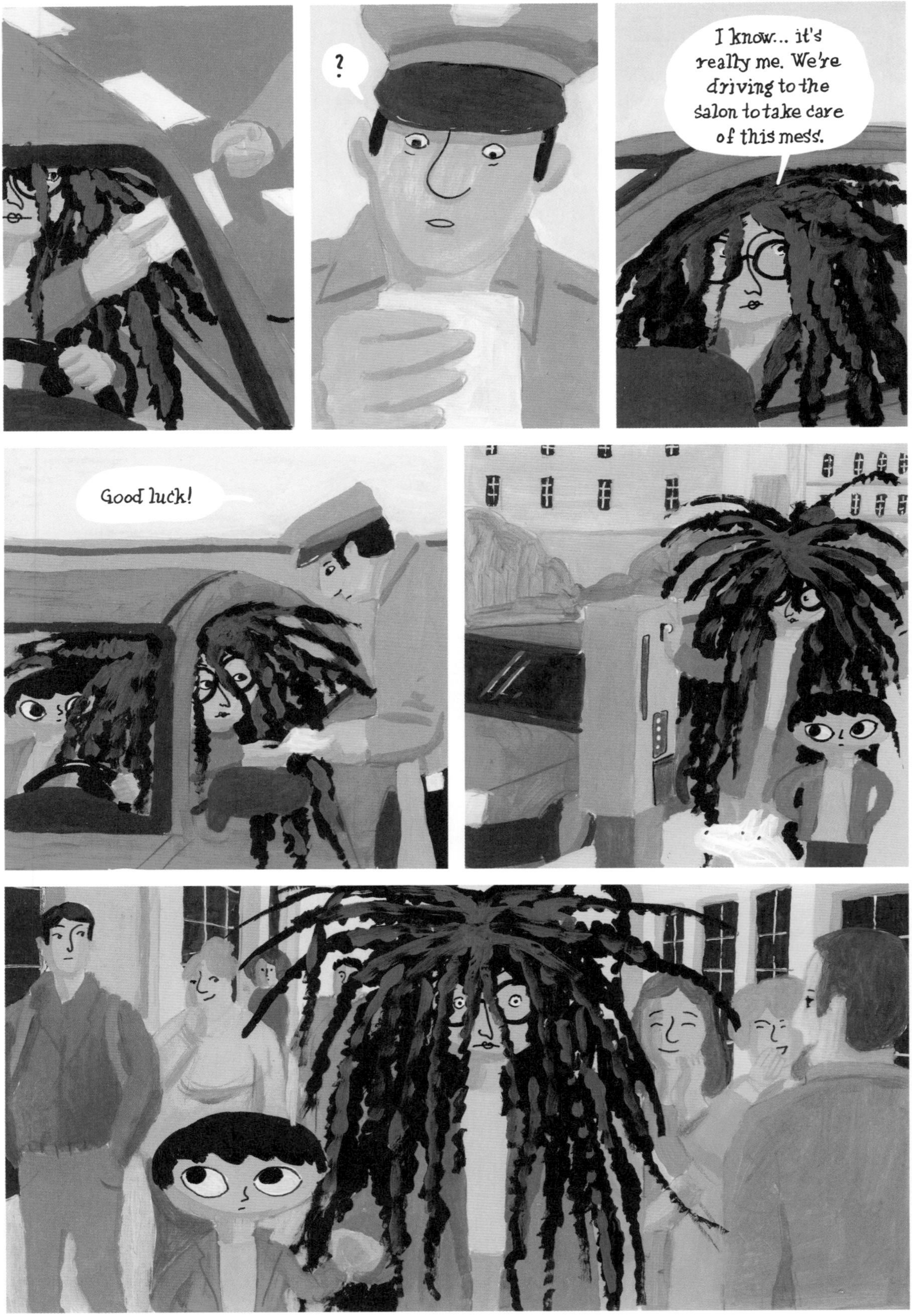
?
I know... it's really me. We're driving to the salon to take care of this mess.
Good luck!

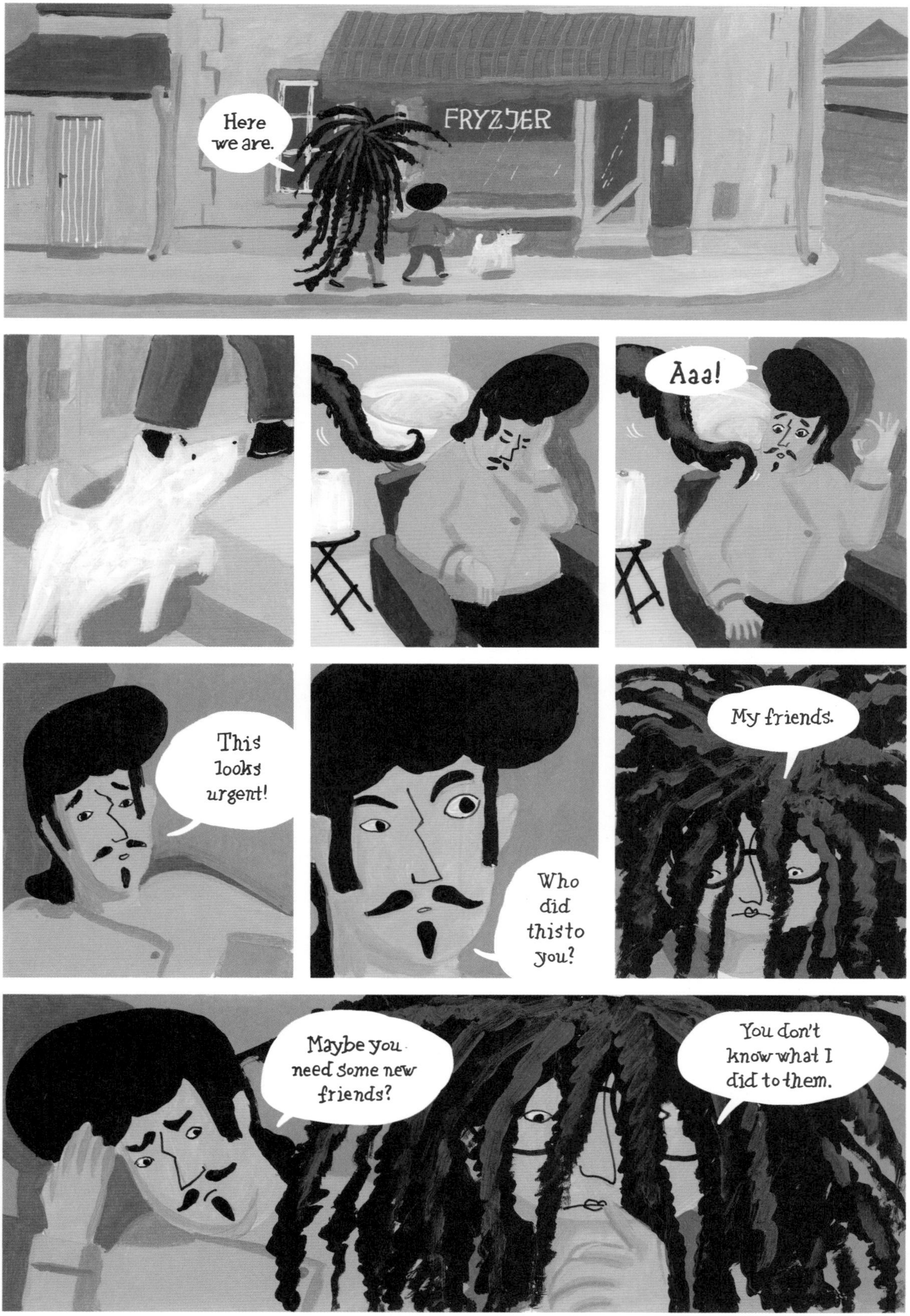
Here we are.
FRYZJER
Aaa!
This looks urgent!
Who did this to you?
My friends.
Maybe you need some new friends?
You don't know what I did to them.

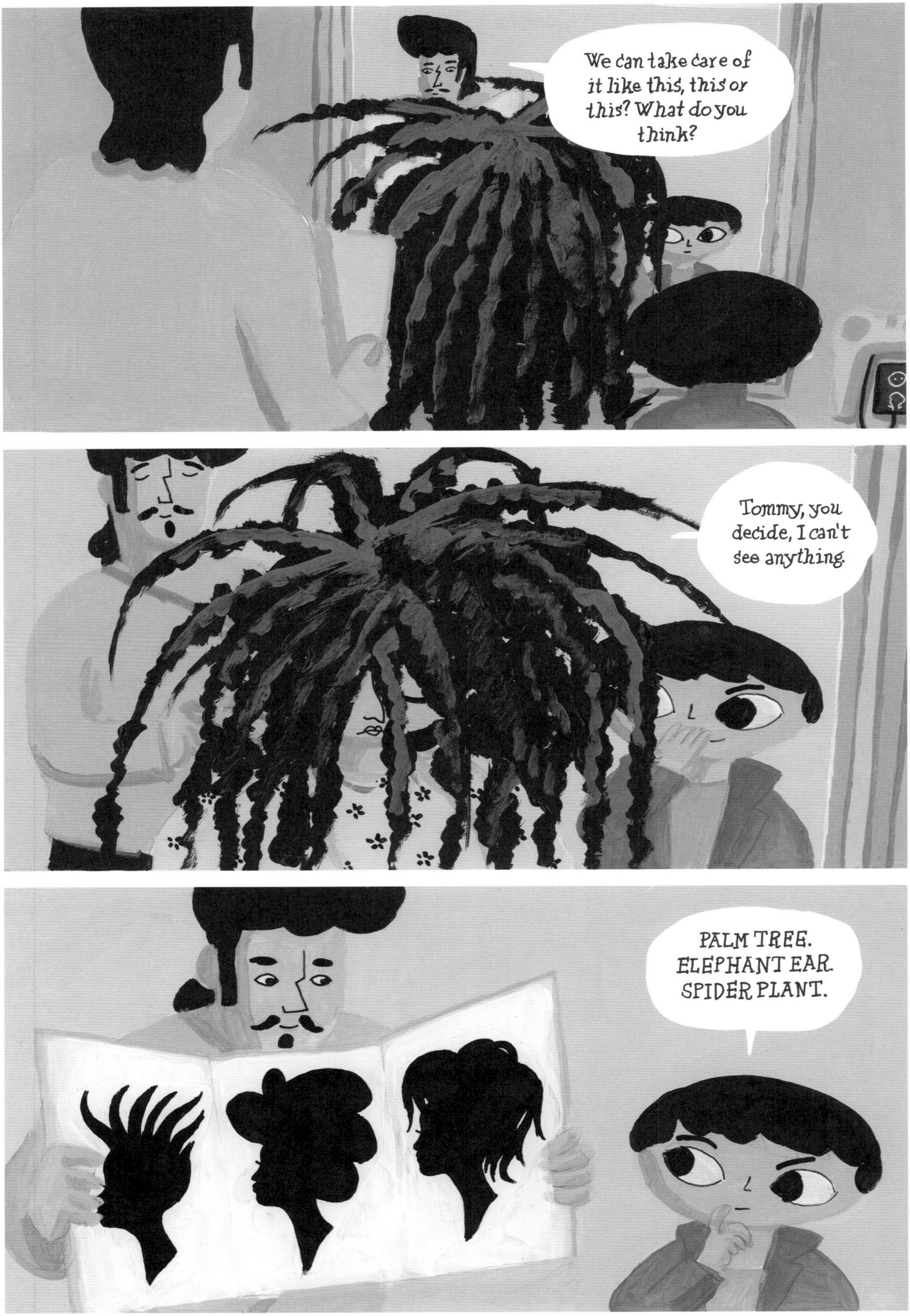
We can take care of it like this, this or this? What do you think?
Tommy, you decide, I can't see anything.
PALM TREE. ELEPHANT EAR. SPIDER PLANT.

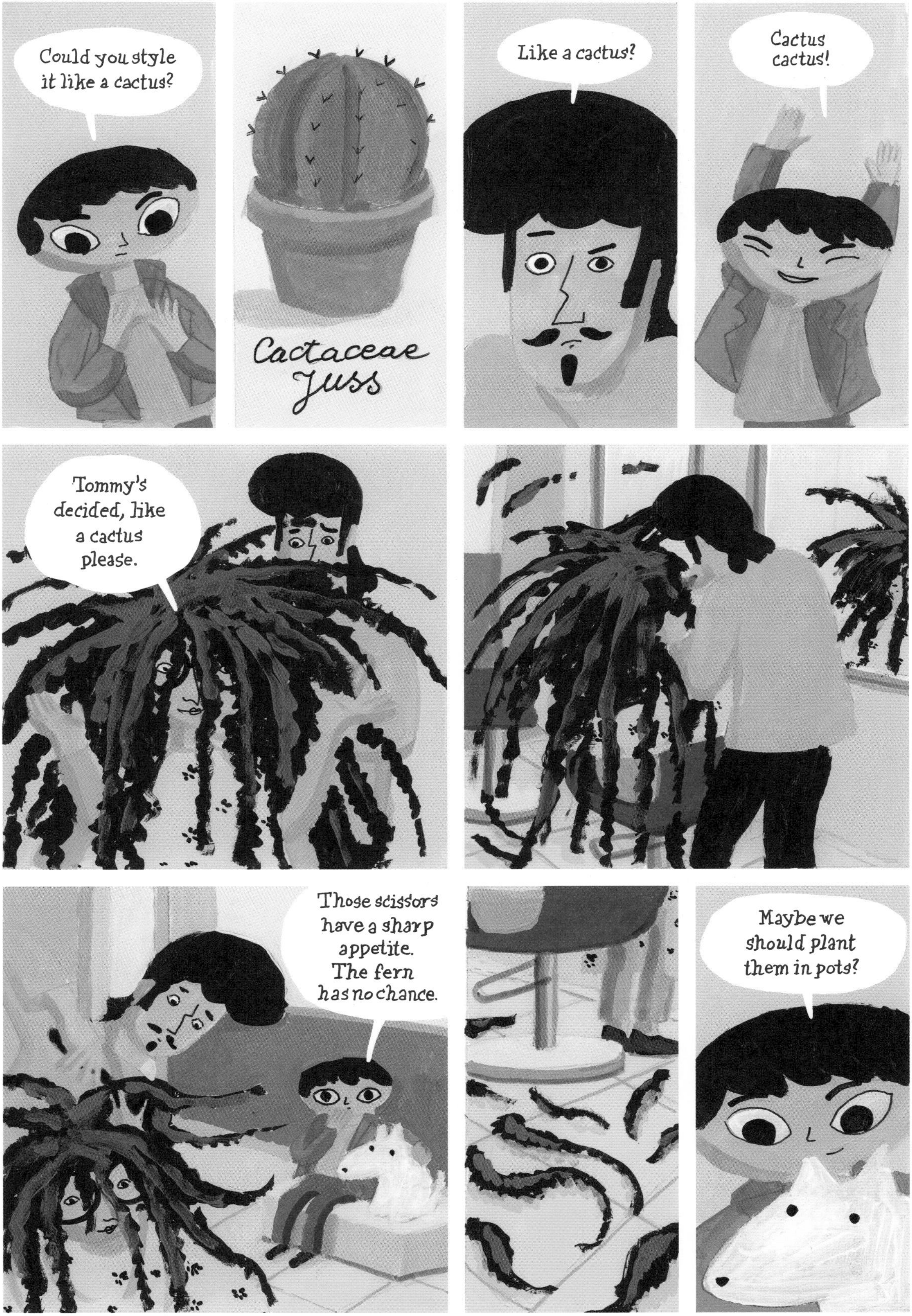
Could you style it like a cactus?
Cactaceae Juss
Like a cactus?
Cactus cactus!
Tommy's decided, like a cactus please.
Those scissors have a sharp appetite. The fern has no chance.
Maybe we should plant them in pots?

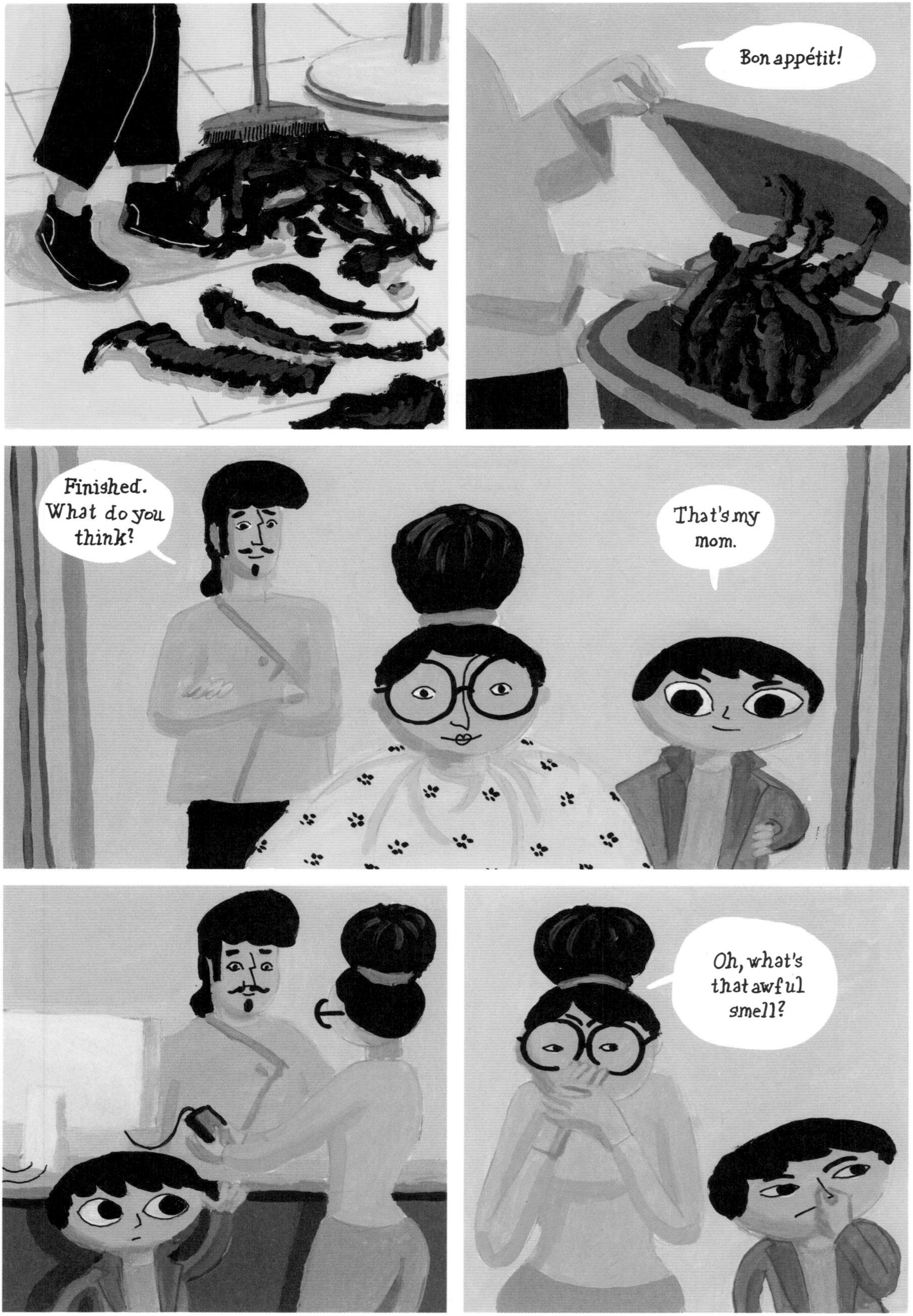
Bon appétit!
Finished. What do you think?
That's my mom.
Oh, what's that awful smell?

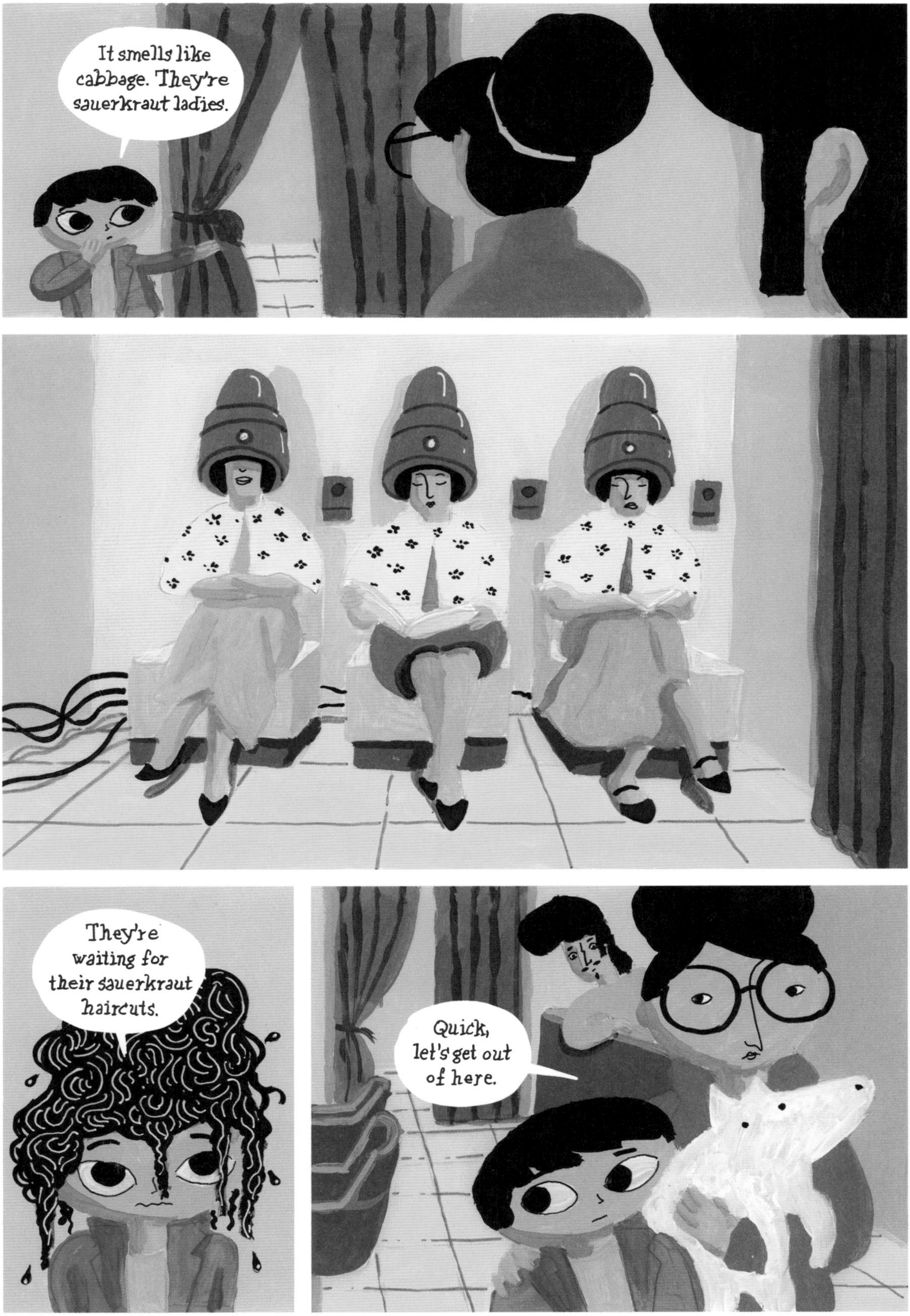
It smells like cabbage. They're sauerkraut ladies.
They're waiting for their sauerkraut haircuts.
Quick, let's get out of here.

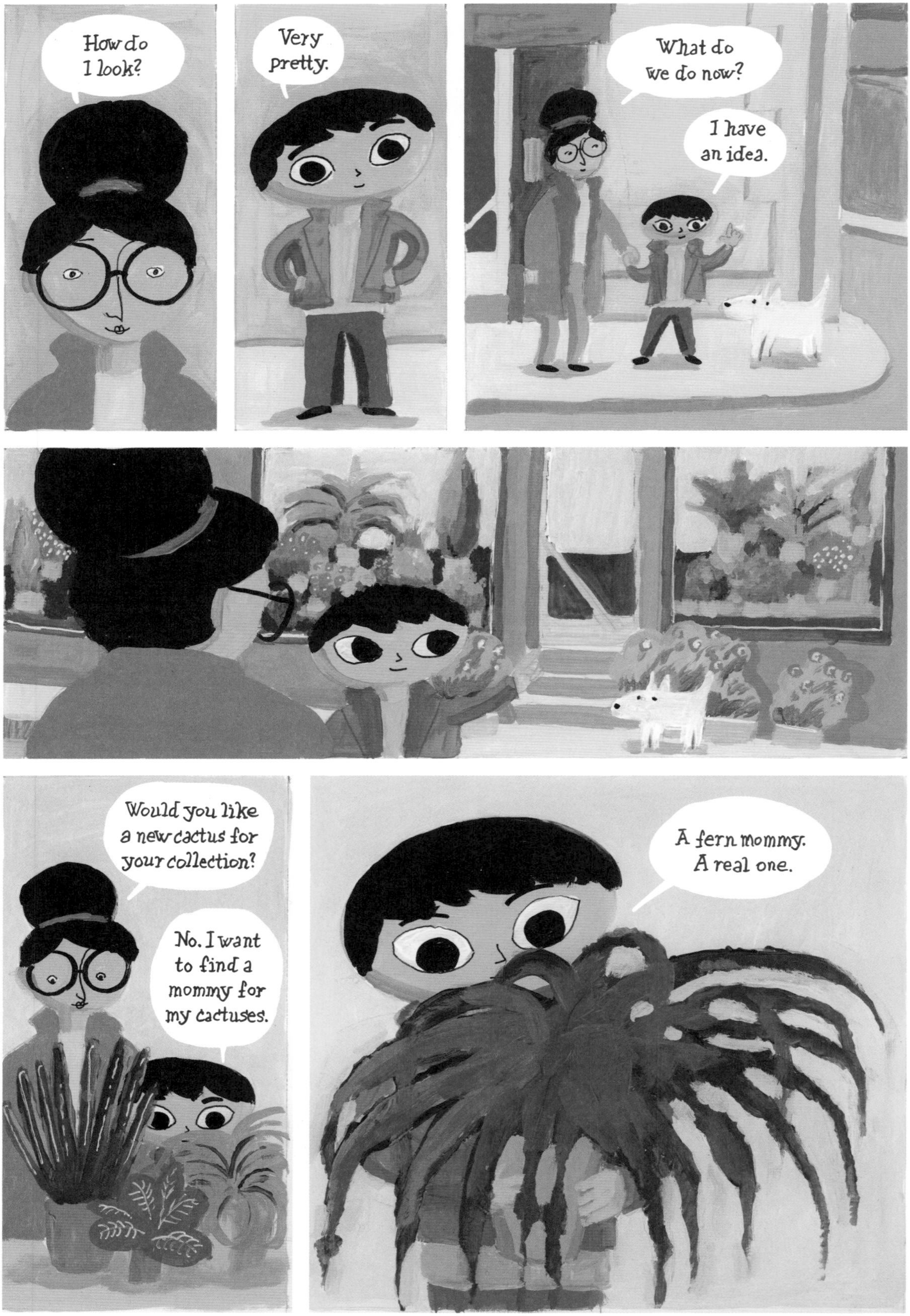
How do I look?
Very pretty.
What do we do now?
I have an idea.
Would you like a new cactus for your collection?
No. I want to find a mommy for my cactuses.
A fern mommy. A real one.

Marzena "Marzi" Sowa is a Polish graphic novelist living in France. She was born in 1979 in the small industrial city Stalowa Wola. She le her country in 2001 and settled in Bordeaux. *Marzi* — her graphic memoir about childhood in communist Poland — was published by Vertigo in 2011. The book has been translated in several languages. Marzi loves dictionaries, is afraid of spiders, and is crazy about skateboarding and cheesecake.

Berenika Kołomycka is a cartoonist, sculptor, and illustrator. In 2011, she received the Grand Prix at the Łodz International Comics Festival. She lives in Poland.

MORE GREAT BOOKS FOR YOUNG READERS FROM:

ODOD BOOKS

MUSNET Series by KICKLIY
NOMINATED FOR THE PRESTIGIOUS ANGOULÊME PRIZE
The Mouse of Monet (ISBN 978-1-941250-09-9)
Impressions of the Master (ISBN 978-1-941250-13-6)
The Flames of the Limelight (ISBN 978-1-941250-15-0)
The Tears of the Painter (ISBN 978-1-941250-13-6)

TSU & THE OUTLIERS
by E Eero Johnson
ISBN 978-1-941250-09-9

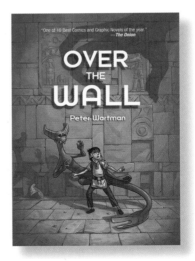

OVER THE WALL
by Peter Wartman
ISBN 978-1-941250-09-9

ODODBOOKS.COM